HIGH ABOVE THE CITY
OF LIGHT . . .

I broke off—and screamed. Behind Méduse, Houdini had suddenly tipped stiffly backward over the railing and disappeared from the platform!

All six of us ran with one accord to the rail and peered over. It made me feel sick to look down so far. All I could see was the great criss-crossing metal leg of the Eiffel Tower sloping away downward. There were no ledges, no projections to break a fall. Houdini must have plunged to the ground.

I guess we were all stunned by the horror of it. Even Méduse. I heard her gasp, "It was only a threat! I never meant . . ."

MYSTERY OF
THE MAGICIAN

BY ELIZABETH HOWARD

ILLUSTRATED BY

MICHAEL WM. KALUTA

A BYRON PREISS BOOK

RANDOM HOUSE NEW YORK

Library of Congress Cataloging-in-Publication Data:
Howard, Elizabeth. Mystery of the magician.
  (My name is Paris) "A Byron Preiss book."
  SUMMARY: Investigating the death of her uncle in Paris at the turn of the cen-
tury, an American teenager meets the famous magician, Harry Houdini. 1. Hou-
dini, Harry, 1874–1926—Juvenile fiction. [1. Mystery and detective stories.
2. Houdini, Harry, 1874–1926—Fiction. 3. Paris (France)—Fiction] I. Kaluta,
Michael William, ill. II. Title. III. Series: Howard, Elizabeth. My name is
Paris. PZ7.H8327Mx 1987 [Fic] 87-4550 ISBN: 0-394-87547-8 (trade);
0-394-97547-2 (lib. bdg.)

Manufactured in the United States of America 1 2 3 4 5 6 7 8 9 0

Special thanks to Michael Hardwick, Mollie Hardwick, Stephanie Spinner, Janet
Schulman, Ellen Steiber, Tisha Hamilton, and Joan Brandt.

Book design by Alex Jay
Cover design by Alex Jay
Cover painting by Michael Wm. Kaluta
Edited by Ruth Ashby

MY NAME IS PARIS is a trademark of Byron Preiss Visual Publications, Inc.

MY NAME IS

PARIS

CHAPTER

1

The French lawyer finished polishing his pince-nez with a silk handkerchief. Then he placed them on the bridge of his nose and picked up the large parchment document from his desk.

It was a spring morning in the year 1900, and I had been summoned to hear the last will and testament of my uncle Claude. Beside me sat my uncle's good friend, Dr. Levine.

The lawyer cleared his throat. "Mademoiselle Paris MacKenzie?" he asked in careful English.

"Yes, monsieur."

"Aged sixteen years, of Chicago, in the United States of America? Niece in direct relationship, of Dr.

Claude MacKenzie, of this city, deceased?"

It had been almost a month since my uncle's death, but there was a part of me that still couldn't accept it. And the reason was plain: I was convinced that my uncle had been murdered. In fact, I'd nearly gotten killed trying to prove it.*

"His only relative now in France," the lawyer went on. "Mademoiselle." His voice pulled me back sharply. "The facts I have just stated. They are true?"

"Yes. Everything you said is true."

The lawyer gave me a half-smile and turned to Dr. Levine. "Doctor, you and your wife have agreed to look after the interests of this unfortunate young lady until her future is decided by her parents?"

The doctor nodded. "That is so. Though I may tell you, *maître,* she has proved more than capable of taking care of herself."

The lawyer was addressing me again. "The will is long and in the usual formal language. If you consent, mademoiselle, I will merely outline the details in simple terms."

"Please, monsieur."

"*Enfin,* there are a good many bequests. The late Dr. MacKenzie has provided cash gifts for each of his servants. Certain items from his dis-

---

* In *Mystery of the Metro.*

tinguished collection of Art Nouveau paintings
and objects are to be presented to museums. Dr.
Levine, you are to receive a number of items
that Dr. MacKenzie had always intended should
come to you in the event of his death."

"I would rather have him alive than receive
his gifts," the doctor murmured.

"There are some other bequests to family
members and friends, including your parents,
mademoiselle. As to yourself . . ."

I hadn't been expecting anything. I was just
there to represent the family. As a matter of fact,
I'd never even met my uncle. Perhaps I should
explain that Uncle Claude was my father's
brother, the only member of the family who'd
remained in his native France. Over the years
Uncle Claude had written me dozens of letters,
telling me all about Paris, the city he'd loved
with all his heart. Then, as a special Christmas
present, he'd invited me to live in Paris with him
for a year. I don't think I've ever been as happy
as I was when my parents allowed me to accept
his invitation. Now I wonder if anything that
promises to be that wonderful actually comes to
pass. I boarded the boat for France, as planned,
and had a fine journey over. But Uncle Claude
did not meet me at the dock as planned. Instead,
I first saw my uncle lying in his study, dead. Of
mysterious causes.

The lawyer was now reading from the will

itself. " 'To my dear niece, Paris MacKenzie, I leave my house, number 26, rue Cambon, together with its furnishings and the remainder of my collection.' "

I felt myself growing giddy.

" 'Appended are details of the income she shall receive in trust until she attains the age of twenty-one, after which . . .' "

I didn't really hear much else. I'd expected to have to return home to the States immediately. Now Uncle Claude had left me the means to remain in Paris—a house and an income.

I was overwhelmed.

Finally the reading of the will was over. Dr. Levine eyed me with concern, thanked the lawyer, and ushered me out onto the street.

"Perhaps you will accompany me for a little walk?" he asked gently. He signaled to his chauffeur, who then proceeded to follow along behind us in the doctor's elegant maroon Daimler. It was a fine spring day, and I was conscious of color all around me as we strolled down the Champs Elysées: blossoms in the trees along the wide sidewalk, flowers in tubs and troughs, and in masses around the flower sellers' stands; the chic Parisian ladies in their bright hats and dresses. Traffic, mostly horse-drawn, swirled along the broad roadway. Everything and everyone seemed alive and purposeful—except me. Still dressed in mourning black, and

dazed by my uncle's bequest, I walked along, trying to decide what was real and what was a dream.

"In spite of the terrible circumstances," said Dr. Levine, "you are quite fortunate, my dear."

"But why *me*?" I finally said. "Uncle didn't even know me."

Dr. Levine shrugged. "He had no wife, no children. You were special to him. He often spoke of your letters. And, personally, I think he could not resist anyone who was named after his beloved city. For any or all of those reasons he made you his heiress. Even scientists can have sentimental notions, you know."

We spoke in French. Three weeks in Paris had done wonders for my high school vocabulary. I might not understand legal jargon, but for everyday purposes I was fluent.

"You see, my dear," Dr. Levine went on, "Claude had everything planned for you. He wanted you to love France and spend as much of your life here as you chose."

"My parents agreed to that?" I asked.

"Your parents wanted you to sample life in the Old World. Perhaps they were not as eager for you to stay here."

I steeled myself. "I suppose I owe it to them to go back."

Dr. Levine regarded me gravely. "I have said before how much I admire your American spirit.

I cannot imagine that you would be happy unless you do what is right for you. The decision is entirely yours, Paris. Remember, it was always understood that you could return home at any time."

I knew that, but even after I'd arrived here to find Uncle dead, I'd never felt tempted to leave. The city of my name had quickly taken a hold on me, despite some experiences I'd gladly forget.

"I do want to stay," I told Dr. Levine. "Besides, if I didn't, what would become of the house?"

"That again is your decision. There would be little point in keeping it on and paying servants' wages if it were left unoccupied. I'm afraid the will has made you a young woman of many responsibilities."

This other side of my "good fortune" was just beginning to sink in. Though I consider myself quite capable, I hadn't had much experience in running a house full of servants.

"There's something else you should be aware of," Dr. Levine continued. "An announcement of the will and a general estimate of the value of your uncle's estate will be published in the newspapers. This may attract unwanted attention from fortune hunters, reporters, and other unsavory types. Though I don't really think there's anything to fear, you will have to be careful, Paris."

But despite Dr. Levine's reassurance, there *was* someone I feared. She was the woman I held responsible for my uncle's death—Madame Méduse.

CHAPTER
2

Dr. Levine took my arm and steered me toward the corner. "You have a great deal to think about," he said in what I took to be a marvel of understatement. "It's time I took you home." He raised his black cane, and his Daimler pulled up to the curbside. The chauffeur got down and opened the door.

As I stepped up I saw something that stopped me and made me turn back toward the sidewalk.

"What is it, my dear?" asked Dr. Levine.

"Oh, look!" I said, and pointed to the wall of a newspaper kiosk.

Gazing intensely at us was a face printed on an advertising bill—a face I recognized from home. Dark-

eyed and handsome, it hinted at something mysterious and indefinable, as if the man who looked out at us knew secrets we could never guess. Over the face ran the words MASTER OF ESCAPE! Below the portrait there was only one word: HOUDINI.

"Harry Houdini!" I exclaimed. "The cleverest man in the world!"

The doctor raised one eyebrow. "Oh? What does this genius do?"

"You've never heard of him?"

"No, but I assume he escapes from something."

"From everything," I told him. "Handcuffs, chains, locked barrels, anything at all. He claims nothing can hold him."

"Is he Italian?" the doctor asked, beginning to sound curious.

"He's American," I said. "Well, actually I think he was born in Hungary, but he was raised in Wisconsin. He used to be a shoeshine boy. . . ." I spotted a smaller bill beside the other and read aloud: " 'For the first time in France, a special Exposition engagement limited to two performances at the Théâtre Robert-Houdin.' "

"Ah, Robert-Houdin," Dr. Levine said. "Now I remember. He was celebrated as a magician in the last century. Perhaps your young man from Wisconsin took a variant of his name, out of admiration." He gestured toward the waiting car. "Well, let's be going."

"Just a moment, please." I looked for the dates of the performance. The first was to be the next evening.

"Dr. Levine," I said as he settled into the car beside me, "I have a wonderful idea. Why don't we all go to the performance tomorrow— Madame Levine, and Rachel and Rebecca—"

"I'm sorry, Paris," he cut in gently. "Entertainment of that nature is quite unsuited to our taste. We rarely visit a theater except for the grand opera or classical tragedy."

Though I am very fond of Dr. Levine, I can't help but feel sorry for his daughters. They are very proper young ladies—which may be more than anyone will ever say of me—but they seem to lead the dullest lives imaginable.

I knew that Dr. Levine wouldn't approve of me going to the theater while I was still in mourning, but I just couldn't give up this chance to see a man whose daring exploits had thrilled America—and me—for years. I would go—and I knew just who I would ask along.

Shortly before my uncle died, two other Parisian physicians also died of mysterious causes. Convinced that my idol Sherlock Holmes would have proceeded quite differently from the Paris police, I undertook an investigation of my own. I suspected that there was a link between the

three deaths and I proved it, though not to the satisfaction of the police. About the only decent thing I got out of the whole difficult mess was a friendship with a young medical student named Marcel Fleury. And, to be honest, we'd become something more than just friends. I admit it— Marcel Fleury was one of the main reasons I wanted to stay in Paris.

"Well, my dear," said Dr. Levine. "I know you can't have come to any major decisions yet, but for the immediate future, how do you propose to go about matters concerning the house?" It was a good question.

"I'm not sure," I said. "Of course, Madame Frenais and the other staff will stay on."

Mme. Frenais was Uncle Claude's house-keeper, a kind and extremely competent woman. She and I had developed an understanding. She was getting used to my American boldness, and I was making a sincere effort to appreciate the finer points of French etiquette. I couldn't imagine running the house without her.

Dr. Levine continued, "Now, as to your uncle's papers . . ."

My head spun with the details. I knew that I would soon have to take a more serious interest in domestic matters. But for now, there was only one thing on my mind—inviting Marcel to see Houdini with me.

"Dr. Levine," I began, unsure of how I was

going to phrase this most improper request.
"Do . . . do you remember Marcel Fleury?"

"I could hardly forget the young man who
defended you so valiantly and almost got his
skull broken for his trouble."

"Yes, well . . . he asked me to have lunch with
him today. To meet him at the *Café Chat Vert*.
Do you think you could drop me off there?"
This was an out-and-out lie, but I knew I could
find my way to the Left Bank, where Marcel
lived, from the café. I crossed my fingers and
hoped that Dr. Levine wouldn't insist on waiting
with me until Marcel showed up.

He eyed me narrowly. "Well . . . perhaps
you've had enough talk of wills and responsibilities for one morning. It might do you good to
have lunch with a friend." He leaned forward
and told the chauffeur to drop me off at the café.
"Perhaps I should go to rue Cambon and inform
Madame Frenais and the other staff of the will's
provisions?"

"I'd appreciate that," I said. "Would you tell
them that I'd be very glad to keep them all on if
they'd like to stay?"

"Of course." The car drew up in front of the
café, and Dr. Levine pressed my hand to his lips.
"Give my best to Marcel. And do not be too
long, Paris. Madame Frenais will worry."

I promised I would be home shortly, thanked
Dr. Levine, and went into the café to pretend to

wait for Marcel. I waited only long enough to make sure that the doctor's car was safely out of sight, feeling a bit like a character in one of my favorite detective stories. As soon as the Daimler had gone, I dashed out of the café onto the crowded sidewalk—and straight into Harry Houdini.

"Pardon me, ma'am," he said, at the same time as I stammered, "Oh, p-pardon me!" It was a wonder he heard me, though, because at this point I was sprawled on the sidewalk in a most unladylike position.

It was only after he'd helped me up that I actually saw him. His hair was longer than it was in the poster, his dark eyes gleamed, and there was the hint of a secret playing at the corners of his mouth. There was something else about him, something a poster could never convey. He seemed more alive than anyone I'd ever met.

I stood there and stared.

"Ma'am," he said, "are you all right?"

I nodded.

He tried again: "*Est-vous* . . . wait a minute, didn't I hear you speak English?"

I nodded again, completely incapable of speaking any language.

"Were you hurt when you fell?" he asked.

"No," I finally managed to say. "I'm fine. Are you . . . Houdini?" Though there was no doubt in my mind, I had to ask.

He looked pleased. "The same. Glad to meet a fellow American, especially such a pretty one."

I thought my knees were going to give way.

"Paris seems full up with us," he went on. "I guess that's why I was booked to come here now."

"Oh," I said, in my most brilliant conversational style.

"What's your name?" he asked, smiling.

"Paris. Paris MacKenzie of Chicago, Illinois."

"Well, I am delighted to make your acquaintance." He bowed low with a flourish and I found myself laughing.

"Now, that's better. Listen, Miss MacKenzie, do you happen to know your way around this crazy city?"

"Sort of. I've been here almost a month now."

"Splendid! Well, then, do you think you could point me in the direction of the Théâtre Robert-Houdin? I'm afraid I got lost on my little stroll, and now I'm late for rehearsal. It's a shame we

didn't bump into each other sooner, because right now I'm afraid I've got to go. I hope you'll forgive me."

"But—"

"But what?"

I didn't really have anything to say. I just didn't want him to leave. "I'm coming to see you perform tomorrow night," I said impulsively.

"Then you're in for a fine show. I've got something special planned for Paris."

"Oh," I said. "Well, if you go straight for two blocks and then turn left, you'll see the theater marquee."

Then he did something that was not at all American, but very French. He took my right hand in his and pressed it to his lips. When he released it I was holding a single red rose.

"Enjoy the show, Miss MacKenzie," he said. He raised his hat briefly and hurried on.

When my heart finally stopped pounding, I remembered that I was going to see Marcel, and set about finding my way to the Latin Quarter. There he shared an atelier—a large, cluttered studio—with his two roommates: Stéphane, a painter, and Paul, a fellow student whose goal in life was to stay in medical school as long as he possibly could.

The Quarter was a fair distance away, so I took one of the horse-drawn omnibuses, riding on its open top. The 'bus trundled past the

Madeleine, a huge, ornate church that looked a great deal like a wedding cake, and across the river Seine. Once again, I felt that thrill as the streets narrowed and filled with a different sort of activity than that of the staid Right Bank. Frock coats and fashionable dresses were the exception here. There were men in striped jerseys and black berets; women in full, workaday skirts and white aprons; and vendors hawking trays of pastries and candies from their carts. Crowded stalls offered food and wine and coffee, and the aroma of it all filled the air. I began to hope that Paul would have his stewpot on the boil.

It felt good to know my way around. I followed the maze of dark, winding alleys that led to the atelier and then climbed the rickety staircase to the top floor. The door was open.

"Paris!" Paul looked up from his stewpot with delight. "What brings you to us in the middle of the day?"

"Your cooking, of course," I teased. "What are you doing here anyway? Don't you ever go to classes?"

"Waste of time," he replied. "I only show up to flunk my exams. They are beginning to despair that I will ever graduate."

"One day they will catch on to you." Stéphane Carrel, wearing a paint-stained smock and the beret which I hadn't yet seen him take off, didn't

even look up from his easel as he spoke. "And no matter how many classes you cut or how many exams you fail, they will pass you just to get rid of you!"

"Marcel," Paul called, ignoring him, "you have a visitor!"

Stéphane put his brush aside, turned, and swept me his usual theatrical bow. "Paris, forgive me for not greeting you sooner, but I was not ready to lift brush from canvas. Come see my painting."

I walked over to the area lit by the skylight and saw that Stéphane had a model posing for him—a dark, gypsy-like girl, wearing a sort of classical drape that seemed to have molded itself to her body. I suppose my only excuse is that I'd never seen a model before, but I couldn't take my eyes off her.

"Paris, this is Carmencita," Stéphane said. Carmencita flashed me a dazzling smile. "Now tell me what you think of her portrait."

For the first time I looked at the painting. Under Stéphane's brush, sunlight streamed into the room, surrounding Carmencita, making her dark skin glow. He'd caught her smiling so realistically that you half expected the picture to break into laughter. Stéphane had taken a pretty girl and made her absolutely beautiful. He came up behind me, laughing. "Maybe you would like to model for me?"

Fortunately—for I might have said yes—
Marcel emerged from the bedroom at that moment.

"Only Carmencita has the patience for you,"
he told his roommate. "Seriously, Paris, he is the
slowest painter in France. He's been working on
this one painting for over a year. . . ." His lips
brushed my cheek in greeting. "What's this? A
rose for me?"

I'd completely forgotten I was still holding
Houdini's gift. "Not exactly," I said. "So much
has happened today. . . ."

"Well, I'm starving," he said. "Have lunch with
us and tell us everything."

Paul served up five steaming bowls of stew,
and we all sat down around the wooden table.
Carmencita, who was now wearing a silk dressing gown, looked like some exotic princess. I
tried to imagine myself modeling. Something
told me that if I were draped in a sheet, the
effect would be a lot different.

"Now, what's the story behind the rose?"
Marcel asked.

"Oh, you'll never believe it!" I said. "Just as I
was going to catch the omnibus to come here, I
ran into *Houdini*!"

The four faces around the table looked blank.

"You mean you've never heard of him? Not
one of you?"

The French may be more culturally advanced

in some areas than Americans, but they had a lot to learn about Harry Houdini. I did my best to fill them in, and they looked politely interested.

"The best part," I finished, "is that he'll be performing tomorrow night!"

This statement caused less excitement than I'd expected.

"Don't any of you want to go see him?" I think I was beginning to sound a little desperate.

Paul came to my rescue. "I am consumed with curiosity to see this marvel," he said quickly. "Mademoiselle Paris, permit me the pleasure."

"You're most welcome," I told him.

"I'm afraid I already made plans," Stéphane said mournfully.

"And I have a sitting tomorrow evening," Carmencita said.

I looked at Marcel, who'd listened to the whole conversation with great interest but had not yet said a word. "I'm thinking it over," he teased.

"Well, then think about this," I said. "The treat is on me."

All three joined in protest at this. It was then I realized I hadn't mentioned the real news. I began to tell them of my inheritance. By the time I'd convinced them I was telling the truth, they were ready to let me take them on a trip around the world. We compromised on the theater instead.

CHAPTER
4

Marcel was due at the Institute for Chemical Research that afternoon, so he and I traveled across the river together in a 'bus.

"Marcel," I began uneasily. "My uncle's bequest . . . does it bother you?"

"Bother me?" His handsome face looked genuinely surprised. "Why would it? All it means is that now, in addition to being naturally beautiful, daring, and charming, you are also wealthy."

"Stop teasing!"

"Paris," he said quite seriously, "what this really means is that now you will always have a home here. I am very happy about that."

Though he'd said exactly what I

wanted to hear, Marcel's earnestness made me feel a bit embarrassed. I reached over and pressed his hand in gratitude—and then changed the subject. We chatted about nothing in particular for the rest of the trip.

I arrived alone at the dignified house on rue Cambon—my house now, incredible as it seemed—to find Mme. Frenais waiting for me.

For the first time, she addressed me as the mistress of the house. "Does Mademoiselle wish the staff to assemble?" she asked, closing the front door.

"Oh . . . no. I mean, Dr. Levine has spoken to everyone, hasn't he?"

"The doctor has made everything quite clear, mademoiselle. Until you make further plans I have instructed the household to carry on as usual."

I felt tremendously relieved. I had no idea how to run a big house and knew it would take me some time to learn.

"That will be fine, madame," I replied, and was trying to think of how to express my thanks when Lucille, the maid, emerged from the kitchen. She held a silver tray with a newspaper on it.

"The afternoon edition, mademoiselle," she said, offering it to me.

"Thanks. That's just what I wanted to see," I said with relief and, taking the paper, headed for my room.

Halfway up the stairs, something made me turn. Mme. Frenais stood at the foot of the staircase, adjusting a picture that hung from the wall.

"Madame," I said impulsively, "I'm awfully glad you're here."

"And I, mademoiselle," she returned. I smiled gratefully and continued up.

I'd been given a big, dark room on the second floor. Now that I had a whole house, I thought I might move into a better bedroom. I settled onto the monstrous old bed and opened the paper. There, as I'd expected, was the announcement of the will. I was relieved to see that neither my name nor the fact that I was in Paris were mentioned, although there was a reference to "a niece from Chicago, USA."

Then there was a knock on the door, and Lucille entered. She held out her silver tray. "Some afternoon post has just come, mademoiselle."

One envelope was pink and addressed in a big, rather scrawly hand which I didn't recognize. It was postmarked Paris, at noon.

It was the other one that I grabbed and hurried to tear open, though. The stamps were American, and there was no mistaking the handwriting. It was my father's.

"Is everything all right, mademoiselle?" Lucille asked anxiously.

I skimmed the letter, smiling. "Everything is just great," I told her. "My parents are coming to visit!"

Papa, who had written the letter, said that they had received a long report from Dr. Levine. It was clear to me that the doctor had tactfully made no mention of my recent adventure. Had they known how I'd traced Uncle's death to Madame Méduse and wound up a prisoner in her laboratory, I'm sure they would have summoned me home. Instead, Dr. Levine had told them how well I was coping with things, and that they could safely allow me to stay on.

Of course, Papa's letter had been mailed before he could have had the full details of the will, but I guess that Dr. Levine, as chief executor, would have told them what to expect. Papa wrote:

You must now face responsibilities which none of us could have foreseen at the time you sailed for Europe. Dr. Levine will provide any guidance and help you might need in day-to-day affairs. The broader future will need more thought, and a lot of discussion among us all. It will be more appropriate to do that on the spot, in Paris, and Mama and I plan to visit you at the first opportunity. We hope you will invite us to sample the hospitality of *your* home!

It was clear that they knew the house was to be mine. I nearly hugged Lucille in my excitement.

"They're coming *here*!" I told her. "Imagine—my parents as *my guests*! Oh, I can't wait!"

"When are your parents arriving, mademoiselle?" she asked. That brought me back to earth. I knew what "at the first opportunity" meant when either of them said it. It was at least three years since we'd even been away together on a family vacation.

"I wish I knew for sure," I answered. "Papa—my father—is a lawyer in Chicago, and his work makes it difficult for him to get away. He has to appear in court whenever he's called, often at very short notice. He couldn't even come and see me off when I sailed from New York."

"But your mother can come?"

I shook my head. "She's almost as busy. She's a doctor, with a lot of patients who absolutely rely on her. They'll come when they can."

"Of course, mademoiselle," Lucille replied. She made a quick curtsy and then left the room.

I opened the pink envelope. There was no address at the head of the sheet of scented pink notepaper, but I knew by the greeting who had written it:

Paris, *Liebchen:*
Regrettable though your uncle's *accident* was,
it is comforting to read that it has placed a
fortune into your hands. I cannot imagine any
other young woman with common sense
enough to control such money. If you should
wish to discuss with me the possibility of
joining forces to develop my important discovery, as well as other projects still in exper-
imental stages, you have only to advertise in
Le Matin. It would then be unnecessary for me
to seek the help of governments, who only
steal brilliant ideas for their own use. Together, *Liebchen,* we could set an example of
success and fame which all womankind would
envy.

Yours again,
Méduse

I could just see her writing it. She was one of
the few people who would have known that the
newspaper piece about Uncle's will referred to
me, and that I was actually in Paris. I pictured
her throwing the newspaper aside and grabbing
for paper and pen. I saw her white hand dashing
the words onto the pink sheet. And I could see
the golden serpent bracelet with its glowing ruby
eyes—the sinister bauble she always wore.

You must understand that although Méduse
was a brilliant woman, her particular brand of
science was not standard. Her greatest discovery

was a nerve gas designed to render enemy troops unconscious—though sometimes its effect went a lethal step beyond and simply killed them. She also practiced hypnotism and something called thought projection, whereby she could project her own images into someone else's mind.

I examined the letter. I knew she was in hiding, and because she had gotten the letter to me so quickly I also knew that she was not far away. Apparently she hadn't given up any of her wild schemes. She was still determined to prove her brilliance to the scientific establishment that scorned her.

I think the only thing Méduse cared for more than her research was revenge. She'd already killed three men for refusing to sponsor her experiments. Now she wanted *me* to sponsor her. The woman was poison.

"Calm down, Paris," I told myself. "Don't let her scare you." I paced my room for a bit. *What should I do?*

At last I decided that the only thing I could do was forget the letter had ever arrived.

So I put on my hat and coat and went out to buy the Houdini tickets as I'd planned. But I hadn't gone two blocks before I felt an all-too-familiar sinking sensation: I was being followed.

CHAPTER
5

It was only about ten minutes' walk to the Place de l'Opéra, where the ticket booth was. It was late afternoon, and rue Cambon and the streets leading from it were almost deserted. All the big houses had their window shutters closed; it seemed they were never opened. How quiet Paris could be!

I quickened my pace a bit, listening hard for footsteps behind me. I wasn't sure whether I actually heard any, or whether it was the echo of my own. I knew better than to look around.

Maybe I was imagining things; but there'd been times before when I'd thought I was being trailed, and I'd been proved right.

By the time I reached the Ministère de la Justice, there were more people on the boulevard. I suppose that was what made me bold again. I had just passed a narrow alley called ruelle Carnac when, about fifty yards ahead, I saw another alleyway. The sign read: RUELLE CARNAC. Obviously, it must loop around, to come out where I'd seen the name first.

I turned sharply into this second entrance and ran as hard as I could. I'd been right. The alley curved back in a wide loop. By reaching the earlier entry I would put myself behind anyone who'd been trailing me.

Very clever, Paris dear! I was still congratulating myself and nearing that first junction with the boulevard when a figure stepped out to meet me. He was short and wiry and lithe and I couldn't have dodged past him if I'd tried. He grabbed my left arm.

"Quickly!" he said in French. "Where is the mirror?"

My voice came out unnaturally high. "Let—let go of me!" I was mesmerized by his face. He had dark hair and skin, and eyes that were nearly black.

"The mirror, mademoiselle." He pulled me deeper into the alley. "I must have it!"

"I don't know what you're talking about!"

He must have felt me trembling, because he eased his grip a little. When he spoke again his

voice was deadly calm. "Now you will stop playing games and tell me exactly where it is or I shall—"

I did the only thing I could think of. I screamed as loudly as I could. Instantly, he had a hand across my mouth. I bit down hard. His fingers loosened and I ran.

He was after me at once. "If only I can make it out to the boulevard," I thought. "Please, let me make it to the boulevard."

Suddenly there was a sharp sound, almost like a whipcrack, behind me. I turned to see my attacker crumble to the ground, his face twisted with pain. And I knew that the sound I'd heard had been a gunshot.

I screamed again. Several passersby from the boulevard came running into the alley, and a few of them shouted for the police.

The man on the ground groaned and rolled over, clasping a shoulder. At least he wasn't dead.

There was more shouting and commotion from the entrance to the alley. I gathered that a gendarme had arrived and was trying to get the excited crowd to make way, but everyone was intent on telling him what had occurred. The wounded man certainly realized as much, and took advantage of it. With a speed that surprised me, he lurched to his feet and tore off down the alley, one arm dangling loosely at his side.

I ran after him, expecting the others to follow. "Stop him! The other entrance!" I shouted, but no one took notice. I heard the sound of feet pounding behind me, and then I was grabbed again and jerked around roughly. There was the gendarme, brandishing a nightstick at me and demanding to know what I was doing.

"It was *him*, not *me*!" I protested, pointing the way the man had run.

The only response I got was a sharp "Keep still!" Then the crowd caught up, and with it another gendarme. He pulled out his notebook and pencil and I knew that that was the end of the chase.

For the second time in my few weeks in Paris, I found myself inside the grandiose Préfecture de Police, near the Cathédrale de Notre Dame. For the second time, I was marched into the frowning presence of an inquisitor, who looked at me as if I were something that had been dredged out of the Seine. Only this time I knew him. He was Detective Latour, who had been in charge of the investigation into Uncle Claude's death. That is, if you could call it an investigation. M. Latour was the sort of man who would make up his mind about something and then look for evidence to prove he was right. It was certainly not the way Sherlock Holmes would work, and I'd told Latour as much. It hadn't helped our relationship.

Now he leaned back in his chair, his hands clasped behind his head.

"Well, well!" he crowed. "If it isn't Mademoiselle Moucharde!" (*Moucharde,* I'd already learned, is an offensive French term for a female private detective.)

"My name is MacKenzie, Monsieur Latour," I reminded him.

"Ah, yes. Take a seat, mademoiselle, and tell me about this 'incident.' "

He nodded to a gendarme, who turned to a fresh page of his notebook and held his pencil ready.

"I was walking down an alley, near the rue Cambon . . ." I began.

"Walking?"

"Well, I'd been running . . ."

"Do you like running up and down alleyways, mademoiselle? It is an American pastime, perhaps?"

I took a deep breath. "I'd been walking along the boulevard when I began to think somebody might be following me."

"Again?"

"Yes, again."

"Why should anyone do that?"

"I don't know."

"If you felt you were being followed along a busy street, why turn off into an alley, where you would be far more easy to pursue?"

"I was doing the pursuing," I explained patiently. "I meant to double back and get behind whoever it was. It didn't exactly work, though."

Latour smiled. "It would take a resourceful man to outsmart you, mademoiselle. Do you suppose he could have been an admirer?"

I felt myself blushing.

"I don't suppose anything of the sort, monsieur. He grabbed hold of me."

I was determined not to let him make me lose my temper, and so I decided to cut the interview as short as possible by volunteering nothing that he might seize on.

"If he was not an admirer, what did he want?" Latour persisted.

"I don't know. My purse, maybe." I was not about to mention the mirror.

"You didn't know him?" His tone of voice insinuated that I did.

"I'd never seen him before."

"Describe him."

"He was small and thin. Around thirty. He looked a bit like an Arab."

Latour raised one eyebrow. "And," he said, "just as this Arab seized you, someone conveniently shot him."

"Yes. Look, Monsieur Latour, I don't know what any of it means."

"No theories this time?"

"Oh, please stop it!" I cried. "If your men had

chased after him instead of asking me questions, *he* could be giving you the answers."

Latour stood up and glared at me. I didn't care. I felt like a cat whose fur has been stroked the wrong way.

"You did not see whoever fired this shot?" he demanded.

"No, I was trying to get away from the man. I didn't even realize he'd been shot till he fell. Monsieur Latour, may I please go now?"

"No!" He slapped his palm on his blotter. "You are holding something back!"

"I'm *not*!"

I guess he decided then that I wasn't going to be much help.

"Very well," he said. "I am tempted to detain you for further inquiries, but I can see no value in it, since neither of the other parties has been arrested. You may go. Please remember, though, mademoiselle, that your antics during these past few weeks have resulted in much waste of valuable police time and effort."

"Thank you very much, Monsieur Latour," I said, swallowing a retort. "I'll bear all that in mind."

He got up and, in that infuriating way he had of suddenly switching from hostility to charm, smiled and said, "Before you go, mademoiselle, I have something for you. Perhaps you would care to take it?"

It was a thick leather-bound volume with brass clasps.

"The late Dr. MacKenzie's diary," he explained. "I took it away to examine it after his death. I have made all the notes I require. You may have it now."

It lay heavily in my hands. Curiosity got the better of me.

"Did you find anything?"

"Nothing to further a suspicion of murder. He recorded no threats against him, nor any unpleasantness."

"Does he mention Madame Méduse?"

"Only what we know—or rather, what you *say*—she told you: that she had approached him with her proposals, and he was not prepared to help her."

"That *is* what she told me, Monsieur Latour."

"I believe you, mademoiselle. The proof is there."

With that parting insult from Latour, I left the Préfecture. I hoped I wasn't going to find myself getting too familiar with it. And the less I had to do with Monsieur Latour, the better!

CHAPTER
6

By the time my interview with M. Latour was over, I'd nearly forgotten about the Houdini tickets. As I set off a second time for the Place de l'Opéra I couldn't keep from thinking about the man in the alley. So far as I could make out, there were three reasons why he might have assaulted me. He could have mistaken me for someone else, another girl with long blond curls and blue eyes who actually had the mysterious mirror. This seemed unlikely, since the man was far too certain I was the one he wanted. Or perhaps no mirror really existed, and the man had been sent by Mme. Méduse on purpose to frighten me. But Méduse

wouldn't order an attack without good reason.

Which led me to the third possibility—there *was* a mirror, and I was the one who was supposed to have it. I just hadn't found it yet.

The day hadn't been an easy one, so it was really no surprise to find a line stretching halfway down the block at the Place de l'Opéra. I took my place, and when, almost twenty minutes later, I emerged with three Houdini tickets, I felt I'd earned a treat.

I decided to take myself to one of the cafés on the boulevards. Marcel, who preferred the small, lazy cafés of the Latin Quarter, would have disliked the one I chose. It was big and bright and very busy. It glittered with color, reflected again and again in glass columns and mirrors.

"Mademoiselle is over for the exposition?" asked the woman who seated me at a pleasant little table. I smiled and nodded, and she took this to mean yes. "Paris has never looked so fair," she enthused. "The lights and displays are magnificent, are they not?"

"Spectacular," I agreed, and it occurred to me that I'd been so caught up in the aftermath of Uncle's death that I hadn't yet toured the exposition. The Grand Exposition was a huge fair—a gathering of exhibits and demonstrations from cities all over the globe. "Soon," I promised myself.

I studied the menu. I had just intended to

order coffee, but when I saw the tall glasses of Russian tea and the cake stands with layer upon layer of pastries, I changed my mind. The waitress fetched one of the stands over, and I chose two creamy things.

"Now, if I were you, I'd take at least three of those," drawled a distinctly American voice.

I turned to see a young man at the table next to mine. He looked to be about twenty-one, with clean-cut, handsome features, slicked-back blond hair, and bright blue eyes. He was immaculately dressed in a blue-and-white striped suit.

"I didn't mean any offense," he said when I didn't answer. "It was just good to hear another American voice." His own accent had a slight Southern cast. He looked friendly and respectable—and nice.

"That's okay," I said. "Actually, you can't imagine how good it feels to meet someone from home."

"Oh, yes I can," he replied. "Ever since I've been here, I've been walking around saying, '*Parlez-vous anglais?*' and most of the ones who do, seem to *parle* the British version."

We introduced ourselves. His name was Franklin Tucker, and he hailed from Richmond, Virginia, where his father owned a string of newspapers. Instead of going to a university to study English literature, he'd gone to work for his father and was now in Paris as a correspondent.

"Then you're covering the exposition?" I asked.

"Not specially. I've written some pieces about it, but I have carte blanche. A lot of people back home are interested in France these days, you know."

He added that he had been in France for nearly three months, making Paris his base but traveling throughout the countryside. Mr. Franklin Tucker seemed to have gotten his life organized in a way that I could fancy for myself. To cap it all, he told me that he had his own automobile.

"Is it a Daimler?" I asked out of my limited knowledge.

"Oh, nothing big and grand like that. Just a Benz. Are you interested in cars, Miss MacKenzie?"

"I like riding in them. It must be exciting to drive one."

"Exciting—and easy."

I remembered suddenly that Uncle Claude's big automobile now belonged to me. Maybe I could get Hector, the chauffeur, to give me some lessons. Frank must have read my thoughts.

"You wouldn't care to try, would you?"

"To drive? Well . . ."

"You could pick it up in ten minutes," he assured me. "Well, maybe fifteen. She's very uncomplicated."

"She?"

"Of course. An automobile, like a ship—like all charming things—has to be feminine. Mine's Daisy. Don't ask why. It just came to me. I think she likes me. In fact, she's waiting just around the corner from here. If you'd care to meet her, maybe I could tempt you to try her out."

I hesitated only briefly. Frank insisted on paying my check with his, and then, with one hand under my elbow, he escorted me out onto the boulevard.

In short order I was staring at a deep green car, gleaming with fancy brasswork.

"Paris, meet Daisy," the proud owner said. "Daisy, this is Paris."

"Oh, gosh," I said. "She's lovely!"

She was, too. She was much smaller than either Uncle's or Dr. Levine's cars, with seating only for the driver and the person beside him. The body wasn't enclosed, and the only roof was a black canvas hood, which had been folded down.

Frank helped me up onto the step and into the passenger seat, then climbed up beside me. I stowed Uncle's diary safely away and then was given a quick run-through of the controls. There weren't very many of them: a pedal, which was the brake; a couple of small levers for increasing or decreasing speed; and an upright steering column with a little wheel on top. The wheel had a

knob to hold and a pointer on its opposite rim.

"See?" said Frank. "All I have to do is spin this flywheel, and the engine's going. I press this lever to release the brakes—you have to pull it to apply them again—and off we go!" As, indeed, we did. I clutched at my hat. We weren't traveling much faster than a man who was walking briskly along the sidewalk, but there was suddenly quite a breeze, sitting up there in the open air.

"It's wonderful!" I cried.

"Next time, have a scarf ready to tie round your hat. Or get a proper motoring veil."

"Yes, I will."

It was only after I'd said it that I realized we had both taken it for granted that there would be a next time. I don't think Frank even noticed. He was concentrating happily on steering us through the traffic, which mostly consisted of horse-drawn carriages.

When we got into the broader Boulevard Haussmann, Frank worked the two other levers—and Daisy took off. My hat was even more imperiled. I held it on with one hand, while with the other I held tight to the little brass rail beside my seat. We shot through the Arc de Triomphe, our engine roaring, and then we were on a far quieter road which stretched out across the beautiful Bois de Boulogne.

Frank worked the levers again. As we lost

speed he pressed down gently on the foot pedal.
We rolled easily and quietly to a stop against the
sidewalk.

"See how easy it is?" He grinned. "Care to
try?"

"Oh! May I really?"

His answer was to get down from his seat and
come around to my side.

"Slide across," he said. "We'll leave the engine
running. Starting up can be tricky."

I moved along the leather seat to the driving
position, and Frank got up to take my place.
Now I felt quite shivery at the prospect of having control of the car. I was glad there was so
little traffic around.

"Concentrate on steering," he instructed. "You
just turn the wheel by the knob, so the pointer
points the direction you want to go. Only slight
movements, though, and not too sudden."

I'd watched him doing it and noticed how
little the wheel needed to turn to change direction.

"Keep your foot near the brake pedal," he went
on. "When you're ready to speed up just say so,
and I'll do the necessary."

"I don't think I'll want to speed up, thanks," I
assured him. He smiled, and motioned me to
work the hand brake. As I pressed it forward he
moved one of the smaller levers and the car began to move. I held on to the control knob as

tightly as I could, keeping my other hand for my hat. By turning the wheel slightly I got us away from the curb.

We trundled along like that for a few minutes, and I began to realize that I needn't be holding the control so tightly. I relaxed my grip and allowed myself to experiment, moving the car farther out into the road, then back a few times.

"You have the hang of it," Frank said. "Ready to speed up now?"

That was a different matter! "Oh, no," I said. "I don't think . . ."

He grinned again and reached for those fiendish levers.

"No, Frank!" I protested. "Please, *no!*"

He paid no attention, just did what was necessary to make the car go faster. My reaction was to hang on more desperately to my hat and tighten my grip on the control again. The wheel jerked and Daisy lurched sharply. I was thrown, screaming, against Frank. He just hooted with laughter and steadied the wheel with his own hand.

"Relax," he said. "You're doing fine."

I doubt if we were going any faster than a man could run, but it felt to me as if we were racing.

"Oh, look!" I cried. We were gaining on a horse omnibus on our side of the road.

"Just pull out and overtake," Frank said calmly. He put his hand on the wheel and gently guided me as I turned it enough to take us clear of the 'bus.

I steered back to the side without Frank's help, and when we started to come up behind another horse-drawn vehicle, I overtook it without his help.

"This beats everything!" I cried.

I soon changed my mind, though. A whole knot of traffic was ahead, moving both ways, and to make things even more interesting, I saw that soon afterward we would reach a crossing, where other vehicles were streaming into the main flow.

"Please, Frank!" I appealed, without daring to turn my head to look at him. To my intense relief he fiddled with the levers again, then said, "Brake!" I jammed my foot on the pedal. Daisy gave a shaking lurch and stopped abruptly, jerking us both forward in our seats.

I felt Frank take me gently by the shoulders and ease me upright again.

"You all right?" he asked.

"Fine!" I gasped. "Sorry about that."

"Don't worry," he said. "You'll remember next time." He was still holding me lightly as he asked, "There will be a next time, won't there?"

"I'd like that, Frank," I answered, and I truly meant it.

CHAPTER
7

It was time I was getting home, so Frank drove me. At my front door he wrote down my address in a neat little pocket book with a silver pencil attached by a silk ribbon. From a pocket in the back of it he drew out a visiting card to give me.

"I come and go quite a lot," he explained. "I'm in Paris roughly half of most weeks, though. May I get in touch?"

"Certainly," I told him.

He was quiet for a moment, then said, "Is there any chance you'd be free tomorrow night?"

"I . . ." Then I remembered. "No. I have tickets to see Houdini tomorrow. With friends."

"Well, now, that's a coincidence," he said. "I was just about to ask you if you wanted to go. I have a press pass for tomorrow night; I have to write about how he goes down with the French."

"You lucky thing!"

"I guess. It's not a bad job." He looked at me as if he was about to ask a question and then thought better of it. "Well, maybe I'll see you at intermission."

"Maybe," I said, and wondered what Marcel would think of this new friend of mine.

He grinned. "Don't forget your book," he said, handing me the diary. We shook hands and I watched him drive away before going into the house.

Lucille opened the door for me. "Some mail has come, mademoiselle," she said. "It was addressed to Dr. MacKenzie, so Madame Frenais told me to put it on the study desk for Mademoiselle to attend to."

"I'll look at it now," I said. "Please ask Madame Frenais if she's free to come and see me there."

I gave her my hat and went down the passage to Uncle's study.

His mail consisted of half a dozen envelopes—notifications of scientific and other professional events, I guessed. I laid them aside to attend to later.

The remaining item was a large rectangular

package, quite thick with padding and with the word FRAGILE stamped in bold red letters in several places. The address label showed that it had come from Sotheby's, the fine-art auction house in London.

I found some scissors in the desk and tackled the thick packaging. I got through it at last, and just as Mme. Frenais came in I drew out from the last layer of folded English newspapers a large, ornate mirror.

It was about a foot high and nearly as wide. The brown metal frame was decorated in the Art Nouveau style with long-legged birds, butterflies in flight, and wisps of tree boughs and grasses. I stood it up on the desk top.

"How beautiful, mademoiselle!" Mme. Frenais commented.

"Isn't it just!" Surrounded by Uncle's collection, I was slowly developing a feel for Art Nouveau. The mirror, I thought, was a decidedly fine piece. "Is it bronze?" I asked.

"No." In her years with Uncle, Mme. Frenais had become something of an expert. "Bronze does not have a luster. This is some form of copper. It will be beautiful after polishing."

Then I found the letter from Sotheby's. Dated ten days before, it stated that the Art Nouveau mirror which Dr. MacKenzie had commissioned them to buy for him at the collection of the late Frau Geisler had been duly obtained at auction

and was forwarded herewith. Their account was enclosed. It had been a pleasure to do business once again on behalf of so valued a client, and they looked forward to being of future service.

No one had sent them word that poor Uncle's collecting days were finished. I sighed and read the letter to Mme. Frenais.

"What shall you do, mademoiselle?" she asked. "Perhaps, under the circumstances, they would find another customer for it."

"No."

Mme. Frenais looked at me in surprise.

"This must have been the last thing Uncle ever bought for his collection," I said. "I'd like to keep it here. It seems fitting. Besides, it's beautiful."

Madame smiled. "Perhaps Mademoiselle would like to keep it in her room?"

That was, in fact, exactly what I had in mind. "Yes, thank you," I said, and then decided that the time was right to ask about something else that had been on my mind. "Madame, about my room. Now that I'm staying on, I'd like to make a change."

"I understand," she replied, and we went off upstairs together.

Uncle had been a bachelor, and there were several rooms in the house which he hadn't used. They looked as if they'd been untouched since Papa and the family left for America in the

1870s. Several had obviously been occupied by the ladies. They were decorated in light, flowery fabrics and furnished in honey-colored wood, with pretty inlays and gilding. One in particular, at the front of the house, had a magnificent bed with a tent-shaped canopy. At the topmost point of the canopy was a big, gilt star.

"Oh, this one, definitely!" I cried. "It's a dream—except that I don't like that dressing table half as much as the one next door."

"That presents no problem, mademoiselle," Mme. Frenais replied. "The dressing tables may be exchanged, as may any other pieces Mademoiselle might wish."

That hadn't occurred to me. It still hadn't sunk in that all this was mine.

"Will you have my things moved, please?" I asked, eager to be out of my own dark, dreary room.

"If Mademoiselle will wait just a little longer, Hector can arrange to have the furniture moved. Then the room can be given a thorough airing and Mademoiselle can occupy it tomorrow evening," Madame replied.

"That's just fine!" I said, and for the next hour or so I kept darting about between the three prettiest bedrooms. Mme. Frenais waited patiently while I decided which pieces of furniture and ornaments I wanted. She sent for Lucille, and told her to bring the new mirror up. I had

just the place in mind for it, on an Empire table with a colored marble top.

When Mme. Frenais and I had finished, I lingered on in my new room. In the excitement of all the arranging and decorating, less pleasant thoughts had been swept away. It was only now, as I looked at myself in the newly polished mirror, that I connected the idea of this mirror with the man in the alley.

"I don't believe it!" I said aloud. Why hadn't I made the connection sooner? Had Sherlock Holmes ever let himself get distracted by interior decorations? "Not likely!" I thought.

I picked up the mirror and examined it. It was a collector's piece but, as I'd learned from the auction-house letter, not worth a lot of money. Certainly not enough to justify shadowing and grabbing a stranger and then getting shot for your trouble. While I knew that collectors often went to great lengths to obtain works of art, I couldn't imagine them scrambling after this mirror.

Perhaps the man wanted it for sentimental reasons, I thought, running my hand over the ornate frame. No, one didn't get oneself shot for sentiment. Perhaps there was something about the mirror that was unique—could it be the work of an undiscovered artist, someone whose talent only Uncle had recognized? Or maybe there was something hidden in the frame. I

turned the mirror over, but could see no way for someone to open the frame, much less hide anything in it. My speculations got wilder. Perhaps there was something in the design itself—a coded message in the way the trees and grasses intertwined or something to do with the number of objects in the design. I actually began counting butterflies. . . .

After about twenty minutes' worth of such hypotheses, I was no closer to unraveling the mystery of the mirror than I'd been when it arrived. The only thing I knew for certain was that somebody wanted it badly enough to risk his life. "If only I could ask Uncle about it," I thought. And then I realized that although I couldn't actually ask him, he might just be able to help. I went down to the study where I'd left his diary.

I opened the leather-bound book, and for a moment it felt as though Uncle were still alive—his handwriting was so familiar from his letters to us in America. I turned to the last pages he'd written. "Must catch the first train to Le Havre in the morning to meet dear Paris," I read. "I do hope we shall be great friends and that this first visit to her family's native land will prove instructive and enjoyable to her. God bless the dear girl!"

Tears filled my eyes. So soon afterward he was dead, without even having been able to greet

me! My handkerchief was quite wet by the time I'd gotten hold of myself.

I had let the diary fall shut, but the thought of the mirror made me open it again to those last pages. I read backward, day by day, until I came to what I was looking for. My heart began to race as I read:

> Heard from London. They have located old Geisler's mirror! His widow had it all the time, and now she has died and her effects are to be auctioned. They asked if I was still interested, and how much I would bid. Telegraphed them by return, instructing them to buy, whatever the cost. I expect they will run me up to a pretty price, to ensure themselves the highest commission. Well, I do not care. I *must* have it, and *she must not*!

There were only two more references to London. One read simply, "No word from London. Telegraphed them to inquire. They replied auction being arranged." The other one, a week afterward, read, "Cannot think why London is being so slow."

I wondered what Detective Latour had made of these entries. Then I realized that they could have meant little to him. They were simply the jottings of a collector who'd been wanting for a long time to get his hands on a certain piece,

had tracked it down, and was anxiously negotiating to buy it.

I was drawn back to the line, "I *must* have it, and *she must not!*" There must have been a woman collector whom he was anxious to cut out. And then, as surely and instinctively as I know where my right hand is, I knew that the woman was Méduse.

CHAPTER
8

I was up the next morning long before Lucille brought in my breakfast tray. I opened the shades and shutters and gazed out across the city.

The sun was glowing through a slightly hazy sky. A thin morning mist clung like white smoke to the taller rooftops and church spires.

"It will be warm today, mademoiselle," Lucille said, putting the tray on the writing table.

"I'm going shopping," I told her. "I want to get a new outfit for the theater tonight. And some clothes that aren't black."

She looked doubtful. "Madame Frenais can send for Madame Vaupin, her milliner friend," she volunteered.

Mme. Vaupin had attended me before, to arrange for my funeral accessories. She had taste and style, I knew, but frankly, we had major differences on the question of what looked good on me. If I thought it was a disaster, she was sure to proclaim it *très chic*.

"Chic," I thought. "What a mystery."

Watching Lucille as she moved about, I realized how well she wore even the maid's uniform. What with the way she carried herself and moved, she looked more up with fashion than I did in any of my American clothes. I guess it's something that comes naturally to French girls.

"Does Mademoiselle know where to shop?" she asked.

"Oh, there are hundreds of places. Everywhere I look!"

"Surely, that will be the difficulty. That is to say, the quality and price of ladies' couture varies so much from one establishment to another. It is possible to walk around a corner and find a garment which appears identical, but is of better make yet lower price."

"You know a lot about clothes, Lucille?"

"I wished to be a mannequin. My mother was against it, but my father allowed me to join a house. I was there some months and learned a good deal."

"You'd be a pretty model. Why did you leave?"

"Men, mademoiselle," she answered frankly.
"Some have too little respect for a working girl.
After two unpleasant experiences, my parents
made me withdraw and enter service."

I had a sudden inspiration. "Lucille, would
you come shopping? Show me the places you
would go to if you were me?"

"Oh, mademoiselle, that would be such a
pleasure. Only . . ."

She shrugged expressively. Her gesture con-
veyed that she was just a housemaid, with duties
to do.

"I'm sure Madame Frenais will spare you if I
speak to her," I said. "I'd really appreciate your
help."

Mme. Frenais looked rather shocked when I
came to her with the proposal. She tried to di-
vert me to Mme. Vaupin, but finally, reluctantly,
agreed.

Thanks to Lucille, I got everything I wanted
in just three shops. First, I bought half a dozen
shirtwaists in plain white linen and cotton piqué.

Black silk stockings were a real luxury to me
after cotton ones. To set them off I chose a pair
of the neat little ankle-boots called *bottines*. For
my other extremity I pounced on an enormous
hat with a wide brim and feathers. Although
Lucille insisted that it wasn't right for my age, I
didn't care. The broad hat made me think of
motoring, and I got two chiffon veils to tie

around it. I couldn't be certain that I should find myself riding in Frank's open car again, but I wanted to be prepared if the chance came.

The pièce de résistance was a debutante frock, simple enough, I suppose, but grand in my eyes. It was in cream satin, with delicate pink rosebuds decorating the short sleeves and sash. I couldn't wait to wear it to the theater that night.

It was after one o'clock by the time we hailed a cab to rue Cambon. Although Mme. Frenais did not look pleased with me for having kept her maid out so long, she only said, "Dr. Levine is waiting for you in the study, mademoiselle."

Dr. Levine was sitting by Uncle's desk, his eyes focused on the closed diary.

"I was afraid I'd lost you to the stores." He greeted me with a smile. "Paris," he continued, his voice suddenly serious. "Latour telephoned me from the Préfecture."

I had known that was coming. I decided to tell him everything.

"It is inexplicable," he said when I was done. "Really, Paris, I think you should have told me all this earlier, instead of running off to shop!"

"But I'm going to see Houdini this evening," I protested. "I *had* to get something to wear for the theater."

Naturally, that didn't impress him much. He gave me an exasperated look.

"I think it is your duty to inform Monsieur

Latour about the mirror without delay," he said sternly. "You have been attacked once, and it could happen again. Besides, we cannot have people going about shooting one another because of something which seems to involve you."

"We don't *know* that it involves me at all, Doctor. It may be all coincidence. Oh, please—if I get in touch with Monsieur Latour he'll have me back in that wretched Préfecture before you can say 'knife.' I detest that place—*and* him!"

Dr. Levine tugged thoughtfully at his little white beard for some moments before responding.

"Perhaps you should show me the mirror and your uncle's diary," he suggested at last. "Just those later entries. There might be something of meaning to me."

"Of course," I said, ringing the bell. "I *was* going to tell you all this, but I thought it would keep until we met again."

"All right, my dear. Just remember that, whatever your feelings about—about certain *individuals*—may be, the police are there to protect you. *And,* when you have something to tell me, Paris, there *is* such a thing as the telephone."

Lucille had answered my ring. I asked her to go and fetch the mirror, which I'd left on my dressing table.

While she was gone, Dr. Levine looked through the diary entries. At last he said, "I'm

sorry, Paris. I'm afraid there's nothing I can tell you. Perhaps when I see the mirror . . ." And it was then I realized what a long time Lucille seemed to be taking. I was about to go off to find her myself when the study door opened and Mme. Frenais came in, with Lucille behind her. I could tell from their expressions that something was wrong.

"What is it, Madame Frenais?" I asked the housekeeper.

"I regret to tell you, mademoiselle, that the mirror is missing."

"Missing?"

"It is nowhere to be found."

I looked at Lucille.

"I went to the blue bedroom," she began, "Mademoiselle's new one, where I had placed the mirror after polishing it last evening. It was not there, and I thought perhaps there had been a misunderstanding when things were being moved to and fro this morning. . . ."

"I could not be everywhere at once," Mme. Frenais snapped. "Lucille was needed. If you hadn't insisted on dragging her shopping with you . . ." She pursed her lips in disapproval.

"All right, Madame Frenais. I'm sorry. Go on, Lucille."

"There's nothing more, mademoiselle. It's gone."

"Have you searched all the rooms?" I asked.

"All of them," Mme. Frenais replied. "That is why we have taken so long. The mirror has disappeared."

"What about the rest of the staff?" I said. "Have you asked Hector?" Hector was our chauffeur-valet.

"Of course, mademoiselle. He helped us search. He is waiting outside now."

"Call him in, please."

Hector, a ruddy, broad-shouldered man in his mid-forties, entered the study, his eyes downcast.

"Well, Hector?" said Dr. Levine, who had known him far longer than I had.

"I can't understand it, Doctor," Hector replied, shaking his head. "I never even handled the mirror, only bigger things. Madame Frenais moved all the small items."

"Did you see it?" I asked Hector.

"I can just remember it, mademoiselle. I haven't much of an eye for things like that, only I asked Madame Frenais if that marble-topped table should be moved to the other room, and she said it shouldn't. I saw the mirror on it then."

"That's right," said Mme. Frenais. "I told them not to move it for fear it might break."

"You told *them*, Madame Frenais?" I asked.

"Hector and the other man."

"What other man?" We had no other male servants.

Mme. Frenais gave Hector a look which indicated that he should answer. I saw him swallow uneasily before speaking.

"Well, mademoiselle, there were some pieces I couldn't move by myself. I daresay if Lucille had been here . . . But since she wasn't, I asked Madame's permission to get help. There was this young fellow leaning against the house opposite, doing nothing, so I asked Madame if it would be all right to offer him the chance to earn a few centimes. Mind you, mademoiselle, Doctor, I passed the time of day with him first, to make sure he was sober and respectable."

"And was he?" I don't know if anyone else noticed the tremor in my voice, but I certainly did. An awful idea was starting to form in my mind.

"Oh, very, mademoiselle. Educated young fellow, but down on his luck. So when I made the offer he fairly jumped at it."

Dr. Levine said sharply, "Do I take it that this stranger was allowed into the house unsupervised?"

"Not at all, Dr. Levine," Mme. Frenais quickly asserted. "He was carrying furniture with Hector all the time."

"*All* the time? Every minute?"

Hector shuffled his feet and glanced at the carpet again.

"Well, nearly, sir. I mean, I had to leave him

for a while, once or twice, to ask Madame
Frenais what we should move next."

"Did you see him leave?" I asked.

"I did. I paid him personally."

"And, of course, you'd have noticed if he had
had anything under his coat. The mirror, for
instance?"

"I looked at him especially carefully, mademoiselle. I looked for bulges in his pockets."

The day which had been going so marvel-
ously was rapidly falling apart.

"Hector," I said, "did you see this young man
again later?"

"Why, no, mademoiselle."

"He didn't go back to where he'd been leaning?"

"No, I expect he went off to buy himself a bite
to eat. He looked as if he needed it. As I said, he
hadn't much strength for a young chap."

"He was thin, was he?"

"Oh yes."

"Thin and small?"

"Quite *tall*, mademoiselle. Outgrown his
strength, no doubt."

"He didn't happen to have a little beard—like
the doctor's, only dark and thinner?"

Although Hector shook his head, looking surprised, and added that the young man had been
clean-shaven, I knew from the sound of Dr.
Levine's indrawn breath that he had realized

what I was getting at. He, too, had thought back to that morning in the Great Gallery of the Louvre Museum whan a tall young artist with a little pointed beard had suddenly become hysterical and diverted the attention of policemen about to arrest an accomplice.

The "artist" had been none other than our real quarry that day—Madame Méduse, in disguise. This episode of the tall young "man" was marked by the same bold style. Méduse had been leaning against that wall, watching the house, wondering how on earth she could slip in while I was absent. Then Hector had appeared, to offer her a chance in a million—and for pay!

CHAPTER
9

"Are you thinking what I'm thinking?" I asked Marcel after I'd finished telling him the whole story.

"Hmmmmm," he replied. He was leaning over a washbasin right in the middle of the atelier, completely absorbed in his reflection as he shaved. I had arrived at the studio earlier than planned and had the unexpected pleasure of watching a young man prepare for an evening engagement. I loved the informality—the way it made me feel at home.

"Actually," Marcel said, turning to me, one cheek still covered with lather, "I am thinking that you look very pretty sitting there in that ivory gown in the middle of this

rat's nest. If Stéphane were here, he'd want to paint you."

Like most French men, Marcel was a born charmer. There were times, however, when I could have done without the charm. I stared at him, wondering whether I should thank him for the compliment or ask him not to change the subject.

"And I am very glad Paul and Stéphane are not here right now," he went on. "Even if all you want to do is talk about that mirror."

"Well? What do you think?"

"It certainly sounds like Méduse's style," he agreed. "What did Dr. Levine think?"

"I don't know. He didn't say anything."

"Didn't you suggest it?"

"Nearly. Then I thought I'd save it to try out on you."

"Well, I'm honored." Marcel wiped the razor on a cloth. "But *why*? What would she want with your mirror?"

"I'd believe anything of that woman," I said, and a shiver ran down my back like a trickle of cold water. "Isn't there something about witches? They steal your nail parings and locks of hair, and so on, to help them gain power over you. I'm sure I read that they like to get a mirror you've looked into, because they have ways to lift your image out of it."

Marcel laughed. "Well, Méduse may be mad,

but that doesn't qualify her as a witch. A murderess and thief, maybe . . ."

"But one who always has a motive," I added.

"Exactly, and motive aside, there's something about this that doesn't make sense. If, as you suspect, she was the one mentioned in your uncle's diary, and she found out that the mirror was coming to you, and sent that Arab to find out whether it had arrived, then why would she have her own man shot before he completed his mission?"

"Maybe she didn't shoot him," I suggested. "Maybe there's someone else involved."

Marcel ran a comb through his black hair. "And maybe," he said, "it wasn't Méduse at all."

"No. The more I think about it, the more certain I am that the 'young man' who helped Hector move the furniture was Méduse. It's exactly her style!"

"It's possible, I suppose," Marcel said offhandedly, "that she wanted to remind you that she has her eye on you. Taking a possession of yours like that might be a warning of how easily she could reach you if she chose."

"Oh, that's a comforting thought." I turned and walked over to the windows. Outside, dusk was falling over the rooftops.

"I'm sorry, Paris." He'd come up behind me. "I was thinking aloud. I honestly can't imagine why she should want your mirror."

"Neither can I," I admitted. "Every theory I come up with is wilder than the last." He turned me to face him, and for the umpteenth time I found myself thinking how handsome he was. "Anyway," I finished, trying not to be distracted, "there's not much we can do about it. We don't know where she is, and I'm certainly not going to get involved with the police."

"Good." He held me lightly by the shoulders. "So we just have to put it from our minds and enjoy our evening." He leaned over to kiss me, and for the moment I forgot about everything else.

"Now," he said, "if you will excuse me, I will go and change so that I look fit to escort you tonight. Paul should be here soon."

He disappeared into the bedroom, and I sat thinking that if I were going to play Sherlock Holmes, Marcel made a somewhat difficult but very romantic Watson. Whatever Méduse might be up to, it was good knowing that I had Marcel on my side.

"Well, what do you think, mademoiselle?" Marcel emerged from the bedroom wearing an elegant, dark velvet jacket over a white shirt. A black cravat was knotted loosely around his neck. Why was it that Americans didn't know how to dress like that?

"I think you'll do."

"That's a relief." He sat down on one of the

rickety chairs. "By the way, I've been making inquiries about your friend Houdini. There seems to be more to him than meets the eye. From what I hear, he doesn't rely on the same old abracadabra to achieve his effects. It seems he can make himself disappear—"

"You mean his escapes?" I couldn't help getting excited about one of my favorite subjects. "Do you know he once had himself locked in a solitary confinement cell? He was handcuffed and they chained his ankles. Then they put him in the cell and locked the door. And just as the officers were walking away they heard a laugh, and they turned around, and it was Houdini walking after them, completely free! No one can figure out how he did it."

"That is what I find intriguing about him," said Marcel. "He must be unusually strong and athletic, and maybe double-jointed, but also he seems to have some extra power that nobody else has."

"Like what?"

He looked faintly embarrassed as he answered. "It may sound ridiculous, but it's said he can dematerialize himself."

"De-*what?*"

"Dematerialize. Make himself vanish, then appear again. When they lock him in a box he turns himself into nothing, then reappears again outside it." Marcel hesitated for a moment.

"Paris, this is all going to sound very strange," he continued, "but in scientific circles, there is talk of something called the fourth dimension."

"You mean like height, width, and depth?"

"Exactly. Only the fourth dimension is time. There are some theorists who claim that all time is one—that the past, present, and future are all going on simultaneously. Do you follow me?"

I nodded.

"Well, these people say that since all time is present, there should be ways to travel through time. If someone were to fully realize the fourth dimension, he would no longer be bound by time or space, but be able to become invisible, fly like a bird, run through the air, into and out of any century."

"What's all this got to do with Houdini?" I asked. "Besides, I thought you'd never heard of him before."

"I hadn't, honestly. But no one spoke of anything else at the laboratory today. Two of the professors had seen him do one of his big escapes in New York when they were visiting. They got so interested that they volunteered to be witnesses. He was locked in a metal tank, and a crane lowered him into the Hudson River. He appeared on the surface in less than a minute, and when they hauled the tank out it was still securely locked."

"I read about that!"

"They are convinced there is no way he could have done it except by using supernatural powers or by entering the fourth dimension."

"But he looks so ordinary," I protested. *Except that he's better-looking than most men*, I added silently.

"I wonder if he somehow hypnotizes everyone into imagining things?"

"I don't think so," I said. "Even if he did use hypnosis, not everyone can be hypnotized." I paused, remembering how easily Mme. Méduse had hypnotized me the first time I'd come upon her in my uncle's study. I must be particularly susceptible to hypnosis, I realized. Then I continued, "There'd always be someone who—"

There was a rush of feet on the wooden stairs, and Paul came bounding in with feverish apologies for being late. He disappeared into the bedroom and returned a few moments later, dressed for the evening. Then the three of us had a quick dinner and made our way across the river to the Théâtre Robert-Houdin, eager to watch the magic and mysteries of the Great Houdini.

I'd heard about atmosphere being electric, and here, in the air of the little theater, it was: you could almost see blue sparks and flashes. The audience was so keyed up that the four-man orchestra was all but drowned out. And despite their continual joking, even Marcel and Paul seemed tense.

"Look at that fellow," said Paul, pointing to one of the stage boxes. There sat a party of young men and women in evening dress. One of the men stood waving, and suddenly I realized he was waving at me.

"It's Frank!"

"Who?" asked Marcel.

"Frank Tucker. He's . . . just a friend. An American."

"I didn't know you had American friends in Paris." Marcel's expression was unreadable.

"No, I . . ." I was about to tell him how Frank and I had met, when I checked myself. I wasn't sure he'd be pleased to hear that I'd struck up a conversation in a café with a stranger and then gone off with him for a motor ride and a driving lesson!

"I didn't think to mention it," I finished, and was glad when soon after the lights dimmed. A hush fell over the audience, and the orchestra actually succeeded in making itself heard.

There was a crash of cymbals and the curtain rose—and Houdini appeared. A great roar of applause broke out as he stepped forward into the blue glare of the spotlight. He was wrapped from head to foot in a black cloak, and he looked taller onstage than he had on the street. Smiling, he bowed to the audience. I hoped he could see me clapping madly.

The orchestra was playing very eerie music

now. Houdini stood perfectly still and then, in one swift movement, whipped off his cloak and threw it into the wings.

There was a gasp from the audience—including me. Houdini was wearing nothing except a pair of black trunks. He stood there like a living statue, all white skin and powerful, rippling muscles. I'd never thought before that a man might be beautiful, but it was the only word to describe Houdini.

"Ladies and gentlemen—friends," he said in English. A young man in evening dress at the side of the stage carefully translated his words into French. "It is a pleasure to be with you tonight. I have here"—he held up a sheet of paper—"a very kind invitation from your Préfecture de Police. They have offered to allow me to try to escape from their newest reinforced-steel handcuffs. And they give me fair warning that no man has ever broken out of them. Very well. I accept the challenge with a respectful warning to the Préfecture that I am a born lock-picker, and I have not yet seen the lock I could not open."

Murmurs rippled through the audience as a tall, beefy gendarme mounted the steps to the stage. When asked by Houdini, he gave his name and assignment in the Préfecture, and assured us that he had checked the handcuffs, and they were in perfect working order. Then from within

his jacket he drew a pair of thick metal cuffs. The house fell silent as he clamped them across Houdini's wrists.

Houdini smiled, a man perfectly content. With seemingly little effort, he snaked his hands about for a moment, then suddenly parted them wide. The handcuffs fell to the floor. He was free.

A roar of admiration went up, and a perfect thunderstorm of clapping.

"It is not possible," Paul muttered. "That gendarme was an accomplice."

But the red-faced gendarme was examining the handcuffs in disbelief.

The translator spoke up. "Many of you will not believe that the gendarme was not an accomplice in this trick. Mr. Houdini assures you that until the gendarme mounted the stage they were complete strangers, and the handcuffs are quite genuine police issue. Houdini invites any other members of the audience to examine them and repeat the trial."

Several did, including a second gendarme with his own set of cuffs, and the result was always the same. Houdini was free of the cuffs in a flash. It was impossible to tell how he did it. I wondered if Marcel was right—did the man have some sort of supernatural power?

Master showman that he was, Houdini knew when to stop. After the fifth demonstration he held up a hand to silence the applause.

"Now I will perform a most remarkable feat. Some of you may have seen it before in this very theater, performed by the great French magician Robert-Houdin. He learned this illusion from an Indian, and it was one of his favorites. Ladies and gentlemen, if I may have a volunteer from the audience, I shall demonstrate to you the wonder of aerial suspension, or levitation."

CHAPTER 10

There was a storm of applause from the audience. I think I must have been the only one who wasn't clapping. I was struggling to get to the end of the row, so I could climb onto the stage.

Marcel tried to pull me back. "Don't be silly, Paris. It might be dangerous!"

"I'll be all right," I called over my shoulder. I just couldn't give up this chance to be onstage with Houdini!

He had wrapped himself in his black cloak, and as I climbed the stairs I thought surely there'd never been a man like this before. Smiling, he held out his hand to greet me. Again I noticed how long and

muscular his fingers felt, almost as if each of them had a life of its own. He recognized me.

"Miss MacKenzie, isn't it?"

"Paris MacKenzie. From Chicago."

"Right."

He spoke to the interpreter, who announced to the audience, "Ladies and gentlemen, this young lady is an American, from Chicago, Illinois."

A good American cheer rang through the house, overpowering the polite French applause.

"Houdini gives his assurance that, nevertheless, he and the young lady are total strangers."

More cheers and applause. I found that, with the footlights and other lighting, I could see no more of the audience than a blur. I smiled down to where I thought Marcel and Paul were.

Houdini kept my hand in his, drawing me up the stage and into the center. As we went he told me, very quietly, scarcely moving his lips: "Don't be afraid, not even for a moment. Okay?"

"Okay," I said. Actually, I was trembling, but it had nothing to do with fear of the trick. It was just that I was standing so close to him.

He took a little medicine bottle from a pocket in the cloak and held it up for the audience to see.

"Ladies and gentlemen, this bottle contains ether. When the young lady sniffs it she will fall into a deep sleep."

That almost panicked me into running back offstage. The recollection of a similar little bottle—Méduse's nerve gas—was too vivid for comfort. I could smell the ether as soon as Houdini withdrew the glass stopper.

"Do you want to remain awake?" he whispered. I gave a barely perceptible nod—and when he held the little bottle to my nose it didn't smell any stronger.

"Seem to sniff it," he ordered, again without letting anyone but me see his lips move.

I obeyed. The bottle smelled of nothing at all. Then I saw, over Houdini's shoulder, a man in the wings holding up a shovel, with something smoldering on its blade. So it *was* all going to be a trick! I was trying, in vain, to figure it out when Houdini said quietly, "Close your eyes." I nearly snapped them shut but I did have the presence of mind to flutter my eyelids a few times before closing them gently.

"Good girl!" I heard him murmur softly.

He led me, eyes shut, to a chair that had been placed at the side of the stage. I sat down slowly and let myself go limp, as if I were asleep. I knew that was what was expected of me, but I didn't expect what happened next. A drum gave a long roll, and then I felt the chair rising, and me with it!

Though I knew that somehow it was all an illusion, I was scared. The audience's gasps and

cries told me that I was several feet up in the air. The chair must have hidden wires pulling it up, but I didn't dare peek. When the chair swayed slightly, making the audience gasp again, I just managed not to grab its sides with my hands.

In a hushed voice, sounding as though he was being careful not to wake me, Houdini announced that he was going to pass a hoop clear around me to prove there were no wires. I could almost feel the audience holding its breath as he did so. I only heard the rustle of his cloak as he moved, and felt a faint swish of the hoop. The audience sighed.

Then the chair was descending again, and settled gently on the stage. I sensed Houdini near me. He whispered "Okay," and touched me lightly on each cheek. My heart pounded. I opened my eyes, shut them again, blinked a time or two, then let them stay open. The applause was deafening.

"All right?" Houdini asked me as the applause continued.

"Was I really up there?" I asked.

He smiled into my eyes. "Of course. Are you game for something else?"

"Oh, yes!" There was nothing I wanted more.

Standing in footlights in my new dress and being cheered like that suited me very well. The stage might not be a bad life. Perhaps if he found

me good enough, I thought, Houdini might ask me to be one of his assistants.

Meanwhile, two men were trundling a heavy wooden chest onstage. They waited beside it while Houdini once again spoke to the audience.

"Ladies and gentlemen, my charming new friend has consented to stay and help me with my pièce de résistance." He indicated me, and I curtsied to loud applause. This was the life!

"It has been rumored that in order to escape from a locked container I am in the habit of dematerializing myself—in other words, turning myself into thin air and presumably drifting out through the keyhole!"

There was loud laughter at this from the Americans, and appreciative applause from the French.

"Well, to give all of you some extra food for thought, I propose to demonstrate how a young lady, who's never done anything like this before, may be locked in this wooden chest, her hands tied with ropes—yet when the chest is opened . . . but see for yourselves!"

One of the assistants tossed Houdini a length of white rope. He gently placed my arms behind my back and fastened the rope around them, not tightly, but definitely tied and knotted. Meanwhile, the assistants tilted the open chest so the audience could see that it was empty.

While Houdini was tying my wrists, he bent

his head to mine and whispered, "When you're in the box, as soon as the lid is closed, here's what I want you to do . . ."

Now, in my opinion the whole point of magic shows is to watch acts that seem impossible and are absolutely beyond us to figure out. Besides, I feel a great loyalty to the magician. So I'm not going to write down what Houdini told me to do. It was quite simple, or he couldn't have trusted me to get it right without practicing. It worked perfectly—but it turned out to have far more sensational results than even he had bargained for!

A little set of steps was put down in front of me. One of the assistants steadied me by the arm, because it's a wobbly thing to do, going up steps with your hands tied. He helped me to climb down into the chest, and then he took the steps away.

Houdini had told me to stand, facing sideways to the audience. He came and stood in front of me and started making passes with his hands in front of my eyes. I'll never know whether he did hypnotize me, as he was appearing to do, but it's the only way I can explain the eerie thing that happened next.

I remember him telling me to crouch down inside the box. I remember that when the drum started to roll, he walked behind the box and picked up a black sheet. Then everything happened at once.

My last sight was of Houdini jerking the cloth up with both hands to hide himself completely from the audience. A second later the chest slid closed on me and I went right into action, doing as I'd been told.

And then—I could *swear* it wasn't more than seconds afterward—I was walking back onstage from the wings!

How I got there I just do not know!

It was like being in a dream, walking back into the glare of the lights, with the audience clapping and cheering like crazy. My hands were free. The chest I'd been in had collapsed into a pile of flat boards and lay there in the middle of the stage, with Houdini's black cloth beside it.

But there was no sign of him at all!

The audience seemed to be cheering me, as well as the trick, so I went forward and did my curtsy two or three times to different parts of the house. It seemed to be what they wanted, but all the while I was expecting the great outburst that would greet Houdini when he came back onstage from wherever he was waiting.

It never came!

I looked around for him. The assistants were out there with me, and they were searching around, too, obviously surprised. I peered into the gloom in the wings, but all I could see were stagehands. They were applauding along with the audience—but now even that noise was fading off. Puzzled murmurs filled the hall.

Perhaps Houdini really *had* dematerialized and was planning on reappearing, out of nothing, right there beside me.

The clapping stopped completely. People who'd stood up to cheer stayed standing, watching the stage. I half expected the drummer to sound off another roll, but he just sat there looking blank.

I didn't know what to do with myself. Should I walk off gracefully into the wings, or down the steps to my seat? My cheeks were burning with embarrassment.

Then, after what seemed like ages, I heard a scuffling noise behind the backdrop. There were people moving, a kind of dragging sound, and a single word spoken sharply in a woman's voice: *"Schnell!"*

I recognized it as the German command for "hurry," and then I realized I'd heard that voice before.

Every instinct told me that the woman who'd spoken backstage was Méduse: the German, the timbre of the voice . . .

It also explained why Harry Houdini was missing.

"Marcel!" I yelled. *"Quick!"*

Then I picked up my long skirts and dashed into the wings.

CHAPTER 11

Men in shirtsleeves and bowler hats blocked my way, demanding to know where Houdini was—as if I was supposed to know! I pushed through them and ran around the back of the scenery, where Marcel caught up with me.

"What is it?" he gasped.

"Méduse," I said.

"Here?"

"I heard her voice. They've got Houdini, I'm certain. We've got to find him before she—"

"Wait a minute." He caught my arm. "This doesn't make sense. What would Méduse want with a magician?"

"I don't know," I said desperately. "But I do know that Houdini

didn't mean to disappear permanently after that last trick and that Méduse had something to do with it. She probably wants him for one of her awful experiments. Oh, Marcel, she could kill him!"

He looked at me doubtfully. "He seems very capable of taking care of himself."

I wasn't going to argue anymore; there simply wasn't time. "You're going to have to trust me on this," I said.

"All right, Paris." He smiled, as if he were laughing at himself. "Let's go find your magician."

At the very back of the stage was a door that led to several flights of stone steps. We raced down as fast as we could, which—thanks to my long skirts—wasn't very fast.

The door to the street was open. Automobiles lined the curb, and about half a block away, there was a small group—two women and a heavyset man, with another man slung across his shoulder—standing by one of the larger motorcars. I recognized it as a Daimler, like the one Dr. Levine owned.

"It's them!" I shouted. "They're putting Houdini into the back of their car. He must be unconscious!"

Marcel had already started to sprint toward them, and I took off after him, wishing that I too were wearing trousers. But before either one of

us could get close, the motorcar pulled away.

"Too late," Marcel said as I came up behind him.

"No, we're not," I said. We were standing right next to a familiar green Benz. "We'll take this one."

"We'll *what*? I don't know how to drive!"

"But *I* do," I said, climbing into the driver's seat. "Hurry, Marcel!"

The black Daimler was still in sight, moving faster now.

"We mustn't lose them," I said, tucking my skirts under me, away from the flywheel. "Please start!" I implored Daisy as I tried to spin the wheel. After only three attempts she obliged.

"Good girl!" I exclaimed.

"Paris—" Marcel began, but I was concentrating.

"Let's see . . . press the lever to release the brake. Done. Now, which of these other levers . . . ?"

"Paris," Marcel repeated, "we can't just steal a—look out!" The brake released with a jerk, and we shot forward, heading into the rear end of the car parked right in front of us. I grabbed the steering wheel and gave it a decisive swing. The car made a sickening lurch, and we were out on the road.

"Paris, what do you think you're doing?" Marcel was furious.

"Please," I said. "I'm borrowing the car, not stealing it. I know the owner, and I'm sure he wouldn't mind. This is our only chance to rescue Houdini. Could you watch Méduse's car?"

"Of course," he said coldly, barely raising his eyes from the hood of the car. This was the first time Marcel had ever been angry with me, and I didn't much like it.

Ahead of us, I could see Méduse's car turning onto the boulevard. I knew that now it would be able to pick up speed.

"Marcel," I tried again. "I don't blame you for being cross, honestly, but can't it wait till later? *Méduse has Houdini!*"

"And his life probably isn't in nearly the danger that mine is." He stared at me in disbelief as I turned onto the boulevard, narrowly missing the curb. "You're improving," he said.

I concentrated on the road and ignored Marcel. The evening traffic on the boulevard was much heavier than by day, and already the Daimler was lost in the congestion ahead. To make matters worse, one of the motorcars had stopped smack in the middle of the boulevard. A chauffeur was worriedly examining its back wheel. Cabbies and coachmen were trying to pass it on both sides, yelling at the poor driver. Naturally, he stood up and started giving back as good as he got. Traffic all but stopped moving.

"Well," I said, since there was nothing else to do, "I guess you want an explanation."

Marcel glared at me for a moment, and then suddenly the old teasing smile was back. "Do you mean to tell me," he said, "that we're just going to sit here and watch this mess?"

"Hold on tight," I said. I guided Daisy to one side of the stranded auto, spied a clearing on the other side, and swerved left. Marcel let out a low moan but, to his credit, did not cover his eyes. "Sorry," I said as we swept past the furious chauffeur.

"Never mind," he muttered. "I'm getting used to it." He stood up now, clinging to the door-side rail to peer ahead. "All this traffic . . . why is everyone . . . there! I see them!"

"Come on, Daisy!" I urged, moving one of the levers a little farther. Daisy picked up speed, and for a few minutes we seemed to fly along. I had the feel of the steering now and found that I could dart in and out of the traffic. We kept Méduse's car in view, and I could tell we were gaining on them.

Then, just as abruptly, traffic again came to a stop. This time it was because we had reached the riverside area of the Grand Exposition. In the bright light cast by the pavilions, I could see throngs of pedestrians crowding the sidewalks and blocking the thoroughfare. A uniformed gendarme had halted traffic and was allowing

only a small group of vehicles at a time to pass through the crowd.

I stood up and peered ahead. The black Daimler was disappearing among those that had just been waved on. "They're getting away!" I groaned.

"It can't be helped," Marcel said philosophically. "If we get stopped for an offense—and in a stolen car—we'll definitely lose them."

Finally the gendarme waved us through as well, but there was no way around the solid mass of vehicles in front of us. I began to feel certain we'd lost out when Marcel yelled suddenly, "They've turned off. Second turn to the left."

"Right. Better sit down."

It was the most difficult maneuver yet. It meant swinging out of our stream of traffic and across the traffic coming the opposite way. I took my foot off the brake and let Daisy loose. It caused a pandemonium of shouts from the other drivers as she pushed in front of them, forcing them to rein in and brake.

We got through, but only in the nick of time. We had just turned onto a narrower side road when Daisy coughed, almost apologetically, and her engine stopped. I was just able to roll her to the curbside before she halted completely. I gave the flywheel a couple of whirls. Nothing happened.

"I don't know what to do," I admitted. "Maybe we're out of gas."

"That's a relief," Marcel said, already getting down. "Come on." He held his hand out to me. "We'll go on foot. No use wasting time."

I jumped down, shook out my skirts, then picked them up and started to run alongside him. There weren't many people about; they all seemed to be on the main boulevard we'd left behind us. It was darker here. The houses were closer together, shutting out the bright lights of the fair.

We ran along for a while until we were both starting to breathe hard. Marcel grinned at me. "Only for you, Paris."

Then we saw it. Behind a tall house, near a long building that looked like a stable, was the black Daimler.

"That is the one, isn't it?" I said.

"I'm certain. Looks empty."

"They must have taken him inside—probably into the stable, because it's so far back from the road."

The iron gates in front of the house stood open. We sneaked through them and up to the car. I could smell the heat from the Daimler's engine. There was no doubt it was the right one. But it was empty.

"Marcel," I whispered. "Go find a gendarme. Back on the boulevard might be best."

"Have you gone mad?" he hissed back. "You think I'd leave you here?"

"I'll just stay here and keep watch."

"You never 'just stay' anywhere. I know you, Paris."

"I'll be okay," I said. "They don't know they were being followed—I think. They're not likely to come out again before you come back with help."

"I'm not leaving you!"

Was Watson ever this difficult? "One of us has to go," I said reasonably. "If they do show themselves again, and I can let Houdini get a glimpse of me, he'll know help is coming. He wouldn't know you."

"I don't like it, Paris."

"Please, Marcel!"

I finally wore him down. He gave me a weary look and, after telling me to be careful, set off.

I moved away from the motorcar, going carefully because the gravel beneath my feet crunched every time I shifted my weight. Finally I made it into the shadow of the stable. I could hear nothing but the distant rush of traffic and some kind of fairground music from the exposition grounds.

I wondered if I should risk getting closer to the stable door, which was shut. Perhaps I should go around the side of the building and look for a way to sneak in.

As it turned out, I had no need to sneak in. A slight crunch on the gravel behind me was all the warning I had before a hand clapped across my mouth and another tightened around my neck. The stable door was flung open, I was given a rude shove, and I made a rather obvious entrance.

CHAPTER
12

Sprawled on the floor of the stable, I stared up into the glittering eyes of Mme. Méduse. "It is always such a pleasure to see you, *Liebchen*," she said. "I have often thought of seeking you out, but now you have saved me the trouble."

I was too shaken to answer her, but stood up slowly, brushing the straw from my dress. I needed a moment to recover, to think. As always in the presence of Mme. Méduse, my stomach clenched, and I felt a sickening mixture of anger and fear. Yet I forced myself to look back at her calmly.

She was as I first met her—tall and slender, dressed like a young man, yet eminently feminine. Her

nose was narrow and aristocratic, her mouth
rather wide and thin, but her most striking fea-
ture was her hair. Jet black, thick and curly, it
sprang out from around her head like a mass of
writhing snakes. There was something both fas-
cinating and frightening about her. And despite
her words, it was clear that she was furious.
Méduse did not like to have her plans interfered
with.

The stable was obviously no longer in use.
There were a few bundles of straw and some
battered tack but no horses. A small gas jet cast
deep shadows in the stalls.

"Perhaps there will be a use for you after all."
Méduse reached out a hand toward me. Instinctively I backed away, but she caught my chin in
her hand. "I think you are just the witness I
need. You will speak on my behalf to your stub-
born countryman." With that she jerked my
head around hard, and I saw Houdini lying on
the stone floor in one of the stalls.

His arms and feet were tied with rope, and his
mouth was gagged. I'd wondered how they had
managed to hold a man who could escape from
cells and strong rooms, and could throw off
handcuffs and fetters as fast as anyone could
fasten them on him. The answer, I saw, was that
a revolver was pointed unwaveringly at his head.
Even the great Houdini wasn't bulletproof.

He was conscious now. Of course, he knew

me; I could see the recognition in his eyes. I hoped he would understand that I wasn't likely to have come here alone.

The weapon was being held by the young girl whom I'd encountered once before in Méduse's underground laboratory. I'd never heard her speak, but Méduse seemed always to address her in German. Indeed, she had a distinctly Teutonic look: her hair was so fair that it was nearly white, and her eyes were cold blue. She looked totally at ease with the gun she was pointing, and didn't so much as glance away from Houdini to look at me.

The man who'd grabbed me proved to be the heavy one we'd seen carrying Houdini. Dressed in evening clothes, he was middle-aged and balding, and looked maddeningly good-humored as he smiled at me before slipping outside again.

"My dear Paris," Méduse said in her soft, mocking drawl, "I should have remembered that you always *do* seek me out. If I did not feel such affection for you, I might term it interference."

"I have no use for your affection," I snapped back. "It's wasted on me." I felt myself shaking inside, even though I knew it was best to act brave.

"Nothing is wasted," she said smoothly. "I told you that we would become allies if you would only help me. Well, now you have another opportunity."

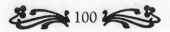

I knew I had to play for time to allow Marcel to return with a policeman.

"What is it now?" I asked.

"Careful, *Liebchen*," she hissed. "Last time you were not nearly as helpful as you could have been. Do not toy with me again."

I swallowed hard. Méduse had wanted me to get Dr. Levine to sponsor one of her lethal gases. Even if I'd wanted to, I couldn't have persuaded him and so I never really tried.

"This time," she said, "you will give evidence to your skeptical countryman. Unless you wish to see him very badly injured you will convince him that I make good on my threats. Tell him, Paris. Tell him exactly what I am capable of."

I looked desperately at Houdini—and heard something outside, the sound of men's voices. Méduse gave me a sharp look.

"Do not think of calling out," she ordered. "You would not like to be responsible for the world's greatest magician being sent to perform in another world, would you?"

"You wouldn't dare!"

"I dare anything to get what I want. Keep quiet now."

After agonizing minutes the voices outside ceased, and the door opened. Marcel came in, looking pale and shaken. The fat man, smiling triumphantly, was behind him; he had Marcel's left arm twisted behind his back.

The man said something in German to Méduse, who gave a short laugh. She evidently ordered him to release Marcel, which he did, shoving him toward me.

"Are you all right?" I cried.

"Fine," he said, but he winced as he rubbed his shoulder. "How about you? She hasn't hurt—?"

"No," I assured him. "She—"

"Both of you, be quiet!" she snapped. She turned to her man. "I gather the police were never notified."

My heart sank. Now we were powerless to do anything to help Houdini. In fact, Marcel and I were in the same predicament as Houdini was.

Méduse spoke to the fat man again, and once more he went out, presumably to resume his sentry duty. I didn't know whether they'd spotted us following them by car, or whether he had been keeping guard and seen Marcel and me arrive. It didn't matter. However it had happened, the situation was very bad.

"So," Méduse addressed me again. "You will now convince your eminent countryman that his life—and yours—are in great danger unless he does exactly as I've asked."

"Does what?"

"That is none of your business. He knows. That is all that matters."

"I'm sorry," I said deliberately. "I can't ask

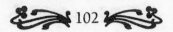

someone to agree to something if I don't know what it is."

"You *are* a difficult child, aren't you?"

"Difficult, maybe, but *not* a child!"

"Of course not, *Liebchen*," she purred. "I meant it only in the sense that you are younger and less . . . less tainted with life than any of the rest of us here."

"Speak for yourself," I said.

Méduse's glittering eyes narrowed dangerously and the half-smile vanished from her lips. "That is enough!" she snapped. "Enough of requesting. You will do what I demand."

"And if I don't?"

"To begin with, I shall recall Max and tell him that your young man here is being offensive to me. Max will know what to do about that."

"Don't listen to her, Paris," Marcel said. "It's all bluff."

Méduse strode to the door. Instead of opening it and calling the fat man, though, she stayed with her hand on the catch.

"After all," she said to me, "it is something perfectly innocent that I ask. It is merely that Mr. Houdini should tell me how he dematerializes himself."

That made me begin to feel there was some hope for us.

"If that's all," I said, "why not ask him?"

Her eyes flashed. "He refuses to tell me."

"How on earth can he tell you anything when he's gagged like that?"

"He indicates that he will not answer anyway."

I shrugged. "It's his secret, after all. Magicians don't give away their tricks."

"Magician! Tricks!" she repeated scornfully. "Who is talking of such nonsense? You know that I am concerned only with the highest sciences . . . with metaphysics . . . with things which I suspect I—and *he*—alone understand."

Maybe I could talk her out of this after all. "Madame Méduse," I said, "frankly, you're wasting your time. Houdini has no more idea how to make himself disappear than I have."

"How can you know that?"

"Simple. I just took part in one of his tricks with him at the theater."

"And?"

"And nothing. It was a *trick*."

Méduse turned impatiently from the door and strode back across the stable. I risked a glance at Houdini. There was a momentary narrowing of his eyes, although he didn't look directly at me, as if he approved of my tactics.

I knew that in carrying out the kidnapping of Houdini, Méduse and her companions could only have seen the first part of the illusion. As soon as Houdini hid himself from the audience with the black cloth, and I was shut into the

chest, they must have gone into action. It accounted entirely for his disappearance: he'd been literally jerked off the stage, made unconscious, and hustled away, evidently without anyone in the wings seeing it happen.

It didn't account for *my* disappearance, though. One moment I had been in that chest; the next, I had been in the wings and had to walk back onstage. I hadn't the faintest idea how it happened; but Méduse and the others had not been around to see my reappearance. They *couldn't* know that there had been a side to the act that was beyond explanation.

"Tell me what happened—in every particular," she demanded.

"Well," I replied, sounding as innocent as I could, "Mr. Houdini told me quietly that as soon as I got down into the chest I should feel for a little hook behind me. I only needed to catch the rope on to it and tug a little and the bonds would untie."

Méduse moved to where Houdini lay and stared down at him.

"Is that true?" she demanded of him.

He nodded.

She swung around to face me again.

"What next?"

"I was to wait till the chest lid was closed. The moment it was I had to press forward with my feet and roll myself backward. Then I was to

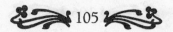

reach out with both arms—like this . . ."

I swung my arms above my shoulders, leaped up, and grasped the crossbeam I was standing under. I drew my knees up and launched myself, legs shooting forward.

My feet hit exactly where I'd hoped—on the blond girl's elbow, smack on the funnybone.

She gave a loud yelp and dropped the revolver.

"Get it!" I yelled to Marcel.

He lunged forward, but Méduse was too quick for him. She kicked the gun and sent it slithering into the darkness of one of the empty horse stalls.

"Max!" she shrieked. *"Komm schnell!"* Then she went diving after the revolver, in competition with Marcel.

I had to let go of the beam as my feet struck the girl. My swing had carried me well forward, so that I landed right next to Houdini. He was working to free himself and I could see the bonds beginning to loosen. Quickly, I untied his gag.

"Thanks!" was all he said before the stable door burst open violently. Max, the fat man, stood there. He had a revolver in his hand, and this time he wasn't smiling.

"Stay still, everyone!" he ordered. He spoke in English, with a heavy German accent. There was nothing to do but obey. But I heard one more of

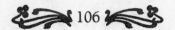

Houdini's secret stage whispers.

"Tower. Eiffel Tower."

Then he let himself slump back to the ground. The rest of us stood up, as Max commanded.

CHAPTER
13

"This is not the moment for any of your tricks," Méduse said menacingly to Houdini. "Your opportunity will come soon enough."

Houdini allowed himself to be slung over Max's shoulder, while the girl kept watch over all of us with her gun. She moved to the door, and Max carried Houdini out. Then the girl slipped out after them. Méduse turned to me.

"As for *your* tricks," she said, scowling, "even my patience has its limits." Her hand moved suddenly to throw something at our feet, and there was a tiny shattering of glass. Then she was gone, and there was only the sound of a bolt being slid across the stable door.

"Cover your mouth and nose!" I cried to Marcel. Gas vapors from the broken vial rose up around us. Holding one hand over his face, Marcel tried to open the stable door, but it wouldn't budge. There were no windows.

"Lie down," he said, and pulled me to the floor near the door. We turned our faces to the crack at the bottom of the door, and tried to breathe the air from outside.

That may have saved our lives, but it wasn't enough to keep the gas from affecting us. Méduse had used her gas on me once before, and I'd had the most terrifying vision of my life. Now, as I felt the walls around me moving farther and farther away, I began to fight it.

"No!" I screamed.

"Shhh." Marcel's hand was over my mouth, his voice gentle. "Don't. You'll take it in faster."

Then the walls of the stable disappeared.

I was lost in an immense darkness.

A disk was revolving, slowly at first, then faster, and I was on an edge of it, whirling around in the emptiness of space. All around the rim there were other people, some familiar, some not, all trying to get off the disk. But they couldn't move. I tried calling to them, but they couldn't hear me. I tried running, but my feet were stuck in place.

The disk spun faster and faster. I realized that if it reached a certain speed I would be lifted off

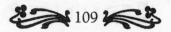

out of space and out of my body—into the fourth dimension.

Lost forever in the darkness.

A handsome young soldier, dressed in a uniform from the Napoleonic Wars, came striding across the disk. I knew it was my Scottish ancestor, the dashing Jamie MacKenzie of the British cavalry. He would help me. He would save me from being stranded in time.

"Captain MacKenzie!" I shouted. "It's me—Paris!" He kept coming toward me, his face getting larger and larger until it filled my whole field of vision. Then he winked one enormous eye, clicked his heels in a military salute, and stepped off the disk and into the blackness beyond.

Lost forever in the darkness.

"Help me!" I wailed. From way over on the other side of the disk, two tiny figures swam out from the dim sea of people and started toward me. They were wearing traveling clothes, and they carried a third outfit between them like a sail. I knew it was for me.

"Mother!" I cried in desperation. "Father!" They floated nearer and hovered above me, smiling. I stretched out my arms to them. They wouldn't leave me here by myself. They had come to take me home.

And then my parents were gone, speeding on past me into that black space. I felt a desolation

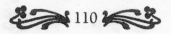

such as I had never known, a void that was both within and without.

Alone forever in the darkness.

I started to sob.

Abruptly, I was in the small, well-lighted study in the house on rue Cambon. Uncle Claude sat at his desk, slowly winding a small enameled clock.

I was not alone after all. I had been saved. I was about to speak to my uncle when the door to the study opened—and Madame Méduse walked in. It was as if I were watching from behind a glass wall; I couldn't hear anything they said. But Uncle offered her a chair, and they talked for a while, calmly, it seemed. Finally, he stood up, shaking his head, and I watched transfixed with horror as Méduse drew a small glass vial from her pocket.

"No!" I shouted. "Don't let her open it!"

At that point Uncle noticed me. Méduse's hand stopped midair as if frozen. "It's all right, Paris," he said. "Time." He held up the clock as if that explained everything. "I can come back any time I like."

Then Méduse was moving again. She opened the glass vial, and my uncle Claude fell to the ground, choking violently. Méduse stood above him impassively, as if she were observing a rat in a maze.

"Help him!" I screamed. "He's dying!"

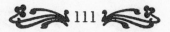

"It's all right, Paris. It's all right." The voice was now Marcel's. He was kneeling on the floor of the barn, holding me as I sobbed.

I felt someone holding my wrist. "She will be well now," pronounced a man's voice in heavily accented French.

I turned my head to see a man with olive skin and very dark hair and eyes kneeling beside me. His left arm was in a sling.

I stiffened against Marcel. "It's him," I whispered, "the one from the alley—the one who wanted the mirror!"

"It's all right." Marcel stroked my hair, trying to soothe me.

"No!" I sat up, wrenching myself away. "He's one of Méduse's thugs. He's—"

"You are mistaken, mademoiselle," the man said. "My name is Risa. I am the eldest son of the Sultan of Rashwar, in Persia. I mean you no harm at all."

"Marcel . . . ?"

"He's telling the truth, Paris. Méduse used her gas on us. Luckily, this gentleman was following her and saw them leave without us."

"How long?"

"You were only out a few minutes," Risa answered. "I don't think she meant it to be fatal."

"No, she never *means* it that way," I said bitterly. "I had the most awful visions."

"I, too," Marcel said quietly, his face still pale.

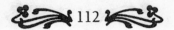

"Somehow I felt sure I'd entered the fourth dimension," I said.

"The fourth dimension!" Risa's voice had taken on an urgency. "How do you know about that?"

"Marcel told me," I said. "Something about time and being able to get right outside it . . . I saw my uncle Claude. . . ."

"Mademoiselle, I must ask again. Have you the mirror?"

I was suddenly weary of all this. "No. I *did* have it, only it was stolen. I'm pretty sure it was Méduse. Do you know who she is?"

Evidently he did, because he said something very violent in what I supposed was Persian. Then he added in English, "It is bad. She will put it to evil use."

"A mirror?" Marcel asked, clearly confused.

Risa looked at us sharply. "Then you did not find the document?"

"What document?" we asked together.

He sighed. "The mirror has a metal backing. You did not remove it?"

"I couldn't even find a way to open it," I told him.

Risa groaned. "Forgive me, mademoiselle, but I have been on the track of this document for so long. I have gone to Germany, to England. I have even been shot." He touched his bandaged arm. "Whenever I think I am on the point of retrieving it, something prevents me."

"What's so important about this document?" Marcel asked.

Risa looked at us as if he didn't expect us to believe a word he said. "It contains a formula for entering what is now called the fourth dimension."

"If that's what I entered, you can have it," I muttered. "It was ghastly."

"Nevertheless, mademoiselle, the secret formula has been guarded by my family for centuries. It is forbidden, under curse of death, to attempt to use it. Over the years some have dared to challenge this curse, but they have always died unspeakably horrible deaths. So few have been foolish enough to try it.

"Then, some years ago, one of my brothers fell deeply and hopelessly into debt in Monte Carlo. In an insane moment he stole this document from my father and sold it to pay his debts."

"Didn't the curse cover that?" Marcel asked with the trace of a smile.

In a toneless voice Risa answered, "My brother was found dead in his apartment less than a week later. He was just twenty-two years old and had been perfectly fit. His death has ruined my mother's health and destroyed my father's peace of mind. I have been sent to reclaim the document so that no one else will be harmed by it."

"That still doesn't explain who shot you," Marcel pointed out.

Risa sighed. "I was aware for some time that I was not the only person on the mirror's trail. Someone else was making inquiries. Since the mirror was not a very special or valuable object, it was obvious that the other person was also after the formula. And unlike our family, that other person would not hesitate to use it to his own advantage."

"No," I agreed. "*She* wouldn't."

"Paris," Marcel said, "I know it is tempting to blame Méduse for everything, but how can you be sure she is behind this as well?"

I turned to Risa. "Can't the fourth dimension be used to make oneself invisible? To dematerialize?"

"Yes, in theory."

"That's enough for Méduse. Don't you see? The rumors say that Houdini can actually make himself disappear—as if he's found his own way into the fourth dimension. That's what she wants from him—the secret of dematerialization. And now, if she's successful, either the ancient document or the master of escape will give her powers greater than those of any other being on earth."

"But Houdini also knows the secret," Marcel objected.

"Not for long," I said. "You don't think

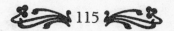

Méduse would allow someone else to share her power? No matter how she learns the secret of dematerialization, Houdini doesn't have long to live."

"We've got to find him now!" Marcel said. And at that very moment two gendarmes, nightsticks in their hands, came rushing into the stable. With them was Franklin Tucker.

"Don't move!" shouted one of the policemen.

"Paris!" cried Frank.

"Frank!" I gasped.

Marcel, looking baffled, stared at both of us.

Risa took things in hand. "You have come to help us find the mirror?" he asked.

"We came looking for my car," Frank said heatedly. "Would you believe someone stole it after the show tonight?"

"Paris . . ." Marcel's voice had a dangerous edge.

"Luckily," Frank went on, "we found it. 'Bout a block away from here. Whoever was driving it didn't use the lights, and a gendarme reported seeing it in this area."

"Oh," was all I could manage.

"Mademoiselle," the shorter of the two policemen said, "it is well known that this house has not been occupied for over two months. What, may I ask, are you and your friends doing in this barn?"

"When we saw the light on, we thought maybe

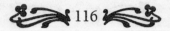

it had something to do with the disappearance of my car," Frank added.

"It did," Marcel assured him.

"Frank," I said, "Daisy wasn't stolen. I borrowed her. And I had a good reason." I gave them a quick version of our pursuit of Méduse. "Now we've got to find them," I finished, "before she kills Houdini."

"And just where will we find this Madame Méduse?" asked one of the policemen.

It was a good question, and all I had to go on were Houdini's last words to me: the Eiffel Tower.

CHAPTER
14

It was not far to the Eiffel Tower, but the traffic was still heavy. We split up into the police cab and the one Frank had come in, both horse-drawn. There was no point wasting time trying to start Daisy up.

Marcel and I rode with M. Dufaur, the shorter and (I thought) more helpful of the two policemen.

"Why the Eiffel Tower?" Marcel puzzled. "How could he know they planned to take him there?"

I'd wondered about that already. "It must have been a threat."

"What kind of threat?" Dufaur asked.

"I'm not sure." I thought hard, considering what I knew about

Houdini and what I knew about Méduse. I had an idea, and I didn't like it. "One of the feats Houdini is famous for," I said, "is being pushed off a bridge with his hands and feet bound. If Méduse wanted to threaten him, it would be like her to force him to better his own stunt."

"You cannot mean that she would push him off the tower?" Marcel said.

"If Méduse thought it would prove or disprove his ability to enter the fourth dimension, she would simply consider it another scientific experiment."

"If he can truly make himself dematerialize," Dufaur murmured, "this is the time to do it."

We were slowly advancing on the tower. I was fairly sure I could have walked faster than the traffic was moving, and said so, but Dufaur advised me to stay put.

I was about to answer him when Marcel intervened.

"Paris, what happened on the stage? I was watching you all the time. You went into the box, and then it collapsed flat and you came back on from the side. Where had you been?"

"Trapdoors," Dufaur told him loftily. "The Théâtre Robert-Houdin was built for such performances. It is riddled with such devices."

"I didn't go through a trapdoor," I said.

"How then?" Marcel insisted.

"I just don't know," I said. I'd gotten out of

the box by doing what Houdini told me. It had been easy; but there was no way I could explain how I'd gotten into the wings.

"Quite simple," Dufaur said sarcastically. "He made Mademoiselle disappear!"

"Don't be too sure you're not right," I told him. It was an uncomfortable thought.

I wasn't able to dwell on it, because we had arrived at the Eiffel Tower, beside the river Seine. I had seen it from a distance often enough—one could hardly have missed a column built of iron girders, rearing up more than a thousand feet, but up close it seemed even more colossal. The base took up several acres of the Champ de Mars and I had to crane my neck all the way back to see where it came to a point far above. The crisscrossing structure was festooned with colored lights for the exhibition, and searchlights played from its pinnacle.

Dufaur explained that the tower was normally open to the public all day, but closed at dusk. Because of the exposition, though, it was being kept open later. Dozens of restaurants, cafés, and shops on the two vast platforms near its base were gaily lit. Music played, and crowds milled about everywhere.

We got out of our cab and were joined by Risa, Frank, and M. Christophe, the other gendarme.

M. Dufaur looked around skeptically. "It is

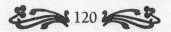

quite impossible that a bound man could have been carried past so many onlookers," he pronounced. "Mademoiselle must be mistaken."

"I am not," I insisted. "Houdini said, 'Eiffel Tower.' Just that."

"That does not mean they intended going inside the tower," Christophe argued. "It might have referred to the vicinity."

I looked at Dufaur. "I told you why I thought they were bringing him here. Why else would they mention it to him?"

"A threat—a bluff."

"All right, then. Where do we search instead?"

The policemen shrugged.

At this point Marcel, Frank, and Risa all said they agreed with me, and since no one had any better ideas, we decided to search the tower.

As we approached it I found proof that we were on the right trail: Méduse's Daimler stood empty, in a line of other motorcars beside the tower base.

There followed a rather long and complicated discussion on just where Méduse was and how we should get to her. We ruled out the main platforms and the viewing platform at the very top because they were all too crowded with visitors. We were sure she couldn't have gone up in the elevators—too many witnesses—or by using the stairs—too difficult with someone who's bound. In fact, it was beginning to look like

Méduse, Houdini, and her entire party would have had to sprout wings in order to reach one of the platforms unseen.

Finally, Risa had a moment of true inspiration. "What is immediately underneath the big platforms?" he asked. "I can see some smaller dark areas. They resemble platforms also."

Dufaur suddenly became excited.

"Of course! They are service platforms giving access to the pipes and wires supplying the platforms. They are not open to the public. Also, they are not enclosed like the larger ones. They have only rails. They would be perfectly suited to what Mademoiselle suggests is taking place."

I could see the little areas clearly, now that they were pointed out. The first level was about a quarter of the way up the tower. It would be an ideal place to threaten someone. No one would survive a fall from there.

We all raced to the elevator gate. A brass indicator showed that the elevator had been to the first platform and stopped there. Frank pressed the button for it to come down, and we made hurried plans.

M. Christophe agreed to remain on the ground in case Méduse or any of her gang should somehow get by us. Risa volunteered to stand guard with him.

"There is also a stairway," Dufaur added. The tower was certainly a complicated structure.

With a little persuasion, Frank said he'd watch the stairway.

That left Dufaur, Marcel, and myself to confront Mme. Méduse on a windy platform above the lights of Paris.

CHAPTER 15

As the elevator rose slowly, the three of us discussed strategy. No one really had a plan, so I improvised. "I'll speak to Méduse," I began.

"And what will you discuss this time?" Marcel asked. "Please, Paris, do not forget the results of your last conversation with her. Méduse is not to be taken lightly."

"I know that!" At the moment, Marcel was not being helpful. "I'll—I'll promise her money for her experiments, anything she wants, if she'll let Houdini go."

"You think she'll believe you?"

"Probably not," I admitted, "but we have to play for time. Maybe Houdini's already started to free

himself. And if not, maybe we can provide the distraction he needs."

"I think this is a terrible plan," Dufaur said. "You will both get yourselves killed. I will simply go in and say they are all under arrest."

Marcel and I looked at the policeman's nightstick. Marcel told him, "They have guns, monsieur. I don't like the plan either, but I think what Paris suggests is safest—especially for Houdini. We've got to let her try and reason with Méduse."

A moment later the elevator came level with the service platform.

The platform was unlit, but the cityscape behind it was so bright that everyone was clearly visible. I took in at a glance Méduse, the fat man, and the blond girl. They were facing away from us, watching Houdini, who stood with his back to the rail at the platform's far edge. He still seemed to be bound, and I wondered if he'd managed to loosen any of the ropes.

Only the girl held a revolver—and it was pointed directly at Houdini's head. Fat Max was securing a coil of rope to one of the girders of the tower's iron leg. The elevator groaned to a stop. Max heard us, dropped the rope, and turned, pulling out his gun. The girl and Méduse had turned, too, and I could see Houdini behind them already at work on the fastenings around his arms.

I raised my hands in a gesture of surrender.

"Madame Méduse," I said, "I have something you want."

Even in the gloom I could see the suspicion in her eyes.

"What is it?"

I drew open the gate of the cage. Max raised his gun, ready to shoot, but Méduse put up a restraining hand. I stepped out slowly and heard the others follow.

"Hands high, all," Max ordered.

"Do as he says," I told my companions. "I only want to talk to Madame Méduse."

"I have had about enough of your talk," she snapped. "And of you."

"It's about the formula," I said. "The one in the back of my uncle's mirror."

That surprised her.

"Wh-what are you talking about?"

"You know, the one you've been chasing after."

"Who told you about that?"

I was getting nervous. "A gentleman I just met. From Persia. He's been chasing after the very same thing. It was his family's property till it got mislaid. He told me about its being in the mirror. I'd never have thought to look."

Méduse came a little closer, trying to make out my expression. She asked carefully, "And have you looked?"

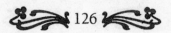

"Well, no." How could I explain this without angering her? "Unfortunately, the mirror disappeared from my uncle's house soon after it arrived from London. Now that I know about the formula, it ties in with some things my uncle had written in his diary, things that concern you . . ."

I broke off—and screamed! Behind Méduse, Houdini had suddenly tipped stiffly backward over the railing and disappeared from the platform!

What happened next was almost comical. All six of us ran with one accord to the rail and peered over. It made me feel sick to look down so far. All I could see was the great, crisscrossing metal leg of the tower sloping away downward. There were no ledges, no projections to break a fall. Houdini must have plunged to the ground.

I guess we were all stunned by the horror of it. Even Méduse. I heard her gasp, "It was only a threat! I never meant . . ."

Frank couldn't have timed his entry better. With all of us turned away from him he crossed the platform silently, tackled Max, and wrenched the revolver from the fat man's hand before he could react. Simultaneously, Dufaur grabbed at the blond girl's arm. She pulled away violently, dropping her gun. It bounced off the platform and over the side.

"Thank goodness," I said weakly.

"Well done!" called another American voice. We all spun around in utter amazement and again peered over the edge of the platform. The great Houdini was very much alive. The ropes that had bound him were gone. Using only his hands, he was holding on to one of the tower's vertical struts. His body hung free in space.

"That rope of theirs," he said. "Let it come over the edge. Make sure the other end's fast, that's all."

Marcel and Frank secured the thick rope. Moments later it swung past Houdini. I almost had to cover my eyes as he calmly let go of the strut with one hand and took hold of the rope. He did the same with the other hand; and then, not even bothering to use his legs, he began to pull himself up. For Houdini it was an easy ascent. Reaching the platform, he bounded over the rail and joined us.

At once we gathered around him, Méduse and her friends temporarily forgotten. The clash of the elevator gate jerked us back to awareness. I was closest and ran for it, but the elevator was already whining downward.

"*Au revoir,* Paris," called Méduse, and she was quickly out of sight.

The blond-haired girl was already gone. Max raced down the stairs after her.

"Stop them!" Dufaur yelled, and we were off. Dufaur headed the chase, followed by

Houdini, Frank, and Marcel. I was last, still wrestling with my skirts. It was a difficult pursuit. The staircase was narrow and steep and seemed to turn at every fourth step. There was no real possibility of overtaking them, and what with the five of us lurching around so, it was too congested and confused for anyone to risk firing a shot.

Max and the girl reached ground level long before we did. They burst through the stairway door, taking Christophe and Risa by surprise. When we finally reached the bottom, Christophe was picking himself up from the ground, rubbing his jaw.

We looked in all directions. Max and the girl were gone, lost in the crowds. The two gendarmes raced after them.

Behind us the service elevator clanked to the ground. I whirled, furious with myself that I hadn't thought to hide and take Méduse by surprise. Méduse took one look at us, laughed, and pressed the button. The elevator started up again.

With a muffled curse, Frank took off up the stairway.

I looked at Marcel wearily. "It's no good," I said. "We can't get up there faster than the elevator."

"All may not be lost," he said thoughtfully, and pointed to the indicator. "Once she gets up

to the platform, she has nowhere else to go."

We waited. A young couple came by and of-fered us extra tickets to the Swiss exhibition. A band nearby played a song about a young man pining for his love. Marcel looked at me and smiled. "When all this is over," he said, "we'll come back and do the exposition properly. We'll—"

The public elevator ground to a stop and he broke off in midsentence, racing to the doors as they opened.

No one was inside.

I was getting discouraged. And then I noticed something. "Marcel, what could have happened to Houdini?"

"I don't know. Do you suppose he went after Méduse?"

"I sure hope so," I said fervently. "Otherwise we'll never catch her."

We waited some more, exchanging increas-ingly ridiculous theories on where Méduse might be. Finally, I couldn't stand it any longer. I had to know what was going on up there.

"I'm going up," I said. "Please, Marcel, stay here just in case she does come down this way."

Before he could protest I was running toward the elevator. I pressed the button and barely squeezed on as the doors closed. "All those peo-ple," I thought, "and not one has the slightest inkling of the chase that's going on around

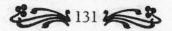

them." We were at the first platform quickly, and I found Risa, Frank, and Houdini all standing around to greet me when I emerged from the elevator. There was no sign of Méduse.

"What happened?" I asked. Three puzzled faces turned to me.

"We don't know," Frank answered. "Risa was here when the elevator came up. . . ."

"But it was empty," Risa said. "She was not inside."

"But she must have been. I watched the indicator all the way."

I turned to Houdini. He looked thoughtful.

"What do you think?" I asked. "You're the escape artist. How does someone get out of a moving elevator?"

"The simplest way," he answered matter-of-factly, "would be through the trapdoor in its roof. One would need to be very quick and agile, but it could be done."

"Do you think she did it?"

He shook his head. "She couldn't have. She'd be visible on the roof outside when the car came up. Our friend here saw it arrive. She wasn't on it."

"Who opened the gates?"

"I did. To inspect inside."

"You said that would have been the simplest way. Are there harder ones, too?"

Houdini didn't answer immediately. "There is

one other way. I could do it. Whether *she* could have . . ."

He stopped himself at that.

"Oh, come on!" Frank protested. "We're wasting time. Where do we look for her?"

Houdini's eyes glittered as he looked out over the streets below. "Where?" he asked, his voice curiously flat. "Anywhere in Paris."

CHAPTER 16

"Thin air?" Detective Latour echoed. *"Rubbish!"*

"There's no other explanation," I insisted. "Even Mr. Houdini can't give us one."

"Not 'can't—*won't.*" The great magician smiled. He pressed the hand of his wife, Bess, who sat beside him on a settee in my drawing room.

We had all gathered there after it had become obvious that any further pursuit of Méduse was futile. She had vanished. Latour, who had been summoned to the Eiffel Tower to take charge, had wanted us to go to police headquarters. Houdini firmly refused, saying that his first concern was for his wife,

who would be frantic to know what had become of him. She traveled with him everywhere, and had last seen him at the theater, just before he vanished.

I didn't want another visit to that grim Préfecture, either, and refused. Frank backed me up. Faced with this all-American majority, Latour had to give in and agree to come to rue Cambon instead. Though it was well after midnight, I telephoned Dr. Levine and asked him to join us. He was the only person I knew who could deal with Latour.

Latour gave Houdini a stern, official look.

"If you have information which might throw light on this matter, monsieur, it is your duty to reveal it."

"I'm sorry, Monsieur Latour, but a magician has a duty that overrides all others. It is to his art, which is as ancient and sacred as any religion. That duty absolutely forbids him to reveal any of its inner secrets."

"You would have answered the questions of those people if you had not been rescued," the policeman said. "They would have made you."

"They would *not*."

"What, when you yourself have told us how they proposed to suspend you from the platform by a rope, head downward, and proceed gradually to fray the rope until you talked!"

A pained look flashed across Mrs. Houdini's face.

She smiled, though, as her husband replied, "No, I wouldn't have talked. I've lost count of the times I've been dangled on ropes. It doesn't bother me."

Frank, who was taking rapid notes for his article, asked, "How did you manage that backward dive off the platform? Everyone thought you were gone for good."

"That's a different form of magic. Acrobatics. A backward cartwheel, to catch on to a strut below. Thirty feet up, or two hundred, it's the same principle."

"You mean, other acrobats could do it?"

Houdini shrugged. "I doubt it."

"Please do not change the subject," Latour snapped. "This woman vanishes unaccountably. It is widely believed, even though you will not admit it, monsieur, that you are able to dematerialize yourself in order to disappear. She abducted you in order to try to obtain the secret of dematerialization from you, but you say she did not succeed."

"Never would have—even if I'd had to drop," Houdini replied grimly, and it made me shiver.

"Then," Latour persisted, "how else could she have vanished?"

"I think I know," I said. "So does this gentleman here."

Risa nodded. "I am coming round to the same opinion," he said. "I never believed it was more than a myth, but now I must think differently."

I told Latour everything about the ancient formula and the strange events I'd been caught up in from the time that I'd met Risa.

"Why was I not told all this before?" the policeman demanded furiously. "You held information back from me when I interviewed you at the Préfecture!"

"Well, only a little, because you were so rude to me. I honestly didn't know how it all tied up together till later—till now, in fact."

Latour turned red. He was starting to look apoplectic. Dr. Levine intervened smoothly.

"Latour, my dear fellow, let us keep calm. Mademoiselle MacKenzie and these gentlemen have been through a most dangerous experience, and Madame Houdini has had a most nerve-racking evening."

Latour seemed about to argue further, but before he could, there was a knock on the drawing room door. Mme. Frenais came in.

"Excuse me, mademoiselle, but I thought you should know at once. This just arrived." She handed me a parcel wrapped in brown paper.

Even before I'd broken through the last layer of wrapping, I knew what it was—the stolen mirror.

Risa gasped.

"Who brought it?" I asked Mme. Frenais.

"We don't know, mademoiselle. There was a ring at the door, but when Lucille answered it there was no one there. Only this, left on the doorstep."

"No one in sight?"

"No, mademoiselle."

"I think this might answer your question." From between the layers of wrapping, Marcel picked up a piece of pink, faintly perfumed notepaper. The writing was in a familiar script:

" 'No hard feelings, *Liebchen*,' " I read aloud. " 'It is quite a pretty mirror, but as I have no further use for it, it would be wrong of me to keep it. Please tell your magician friend that it was a privilege to witness his daring trick this evening. I hope he appreciated mine.' "

"Indeed," Houdini said with a chuckle.

I held up the mirror and examined it carefully. Still, I could see no way for it to open. I gave it to Risa.

He held the mirror with a kind of reverence, carefully going over every inch of the frame. I half think he didn't want it to open, didn't want to find out that Méduse had taken the precious document.

At last he looked up. "It has all been for nothing," he said slowly. "I have been led on a wild chase. This frame could not hide what I have been searching for. It does not open."

Houdini crossed the room toward him. "Mind if I try?" he asked. Risa shrugged and gave him the mirror.

As we had, Houdini held the mirror up and examined it from both sides. "A clever piece of work," he said, then pressed against the left side of the frame. The back sprang open. "I believe this is what you were looking for," he said calmly, and handed Risa a small piece of yellowed parchment. Whatever the paper contained must have been important, for surrounding the Arabic lettering was a beautiful painted border, illuminated in green and gold.

Risa's hands shook as he held the object he'd searched all of Europe to find. "I thank you, all of you," he said simply. "I have fulfilled my duty to my family."

"I think there's another story here," said Frank.

"Ah, but this one ends in mystery," Houdini added with obvious relish. "To begin with, was Méduse ever able to open the mirror? And if she did, could she have read the document? Copied it perhaps? Did she then replace it? Perhaps most interesting of all, did she in fact learn to travel into the fourth dimension?" He paused dramatically. "Only the mirror knows the answers to these questions."

He stood up, gave a mock showman's bow, and then, with a conspirator's wink, addressed the mirror itself. "And as we all know, a good secret is never revealed."

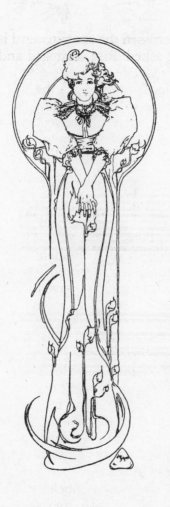